Classic Curves

WHISKEY SURPRISES

JAQUELINE SNOWE

Whiskey Surprises
ISBN # 978-1-83943-836-3
©Copyright Jaqueline Snowe 2019
Cover Art by Erin Dameron-Hill ©Copyright June 2019
Interior text design by Claire Siemaszkiewicz
Totally Bound Publishing

Published in 2019 by Totally Bound Publishing, United Kingdom.

WHISKEY
SURPRISES

Dedication

To the BG team and all the Fireball. Those
summers together will always be some of my
favorite memories.

To my mom and Cathy and all the giggles. You're
both badass ladies and I love you for it.

To Rebecca. As always, working with you is
nothing short of amazing.

Chapter One

Fern

It didn't matter how many damn to-do lists I had, or how many of those items I checked off—I could never sleep the night before the big event. My Rusty Nail, the best drink ever created, burned my throat in the perfect way and the adorable bartender slid me my second glass. He defined eye-candy with his plucked eyebrows, chiseled jaw and styled hair, a bit too young for the looks he was throwing my way. I had no issues with being a cougar, but there were lines I wouldn't cross. He was one of them.

He flipped the towel in a dramatic fashion and I hid my snort. In a practiced move perfected by long nights with big tippers, he leaned over the bar onto his strong arms and batted his long lashes. He dipped his head slightly to the side and met my gaze. "Mama, what's a pretty thing like you doing sitting at a bar alone?"

"Drinking. Strong, independent women are the new wave." I scanned for a name tag and not at all over his uber-defined pecs. Tony grinned but leaned closer and crooked his finger for me to lean in. I wasn't rude, so I appeased him.

"You must have a lot of confidence to sit alone."

I tilted my head to the opposite angle and added a bit of attitude to my voice. "Incorrect. I have a lot of desire to *drink* alone." I held up the glass. "Cheers, Tony."

He got the hint and took his charm elsewhere. I closed my eyes and hummed in pleasure at the rich taste of Scottish whiskey and Drambuie. The honey and citrus combination almost calmed the nerves dancing around in my belly. Some people handled pressure fine. I did not. Stress began in my gut and spread throughout my limbs, making me second-guess every decision I had made regarding the event. *Every* decision. Like, why didn't I order red polo shirts for the staff? Did I bring enough socks for the week?

Right, it didn't matter. But my nerves got the better of me and whiskey was the answer to any question. I took another sip, the pain in my chest growing at the severity of my situation. I pinched the bridge of my nose, hoping to relieve some of my tension, but failed. I continued to replay my boss's words. If I said them enough, then maybe they wouldn't be true — if we didn't make our threshold in revenue this year, then I wouldn't have a job.

Being single at thirty-two when every goddamn person I knew had two-point-five kids and a house with four dogs and a partner was annoying. I loved my friends, coworkers, family — the whole lot of them. Even my younger brother who rarely showered had found a human who wanted to spend his life with him. I could handle their jabs about my personal life and if I was confused. But being single *and* unemployed was not a route I wanted to head down. *Nope. No thank you.*

It wasn't as if I was awful or un-dateable. I took care of myself, ate healthily, worked out and had a normal amount of confidence and above-average conversational skills. I just didn't like wasting time on small talk when I had to help run a multimillion-dollar Silvas car show. *Ain't no time for relationships when a wild ride in the sack suffices.* Plus, why force a relationship if I knew it wasn't going to work?

"You look like you're trying to solve all the world's problems," someone said next to me. The voice deep, a guttural masculine rhythm. It startled me a bit and I set my glass on the bar before giving the stranger my attention.

"Try again."

"Excuse me?" His deep voice drew me in, instantly sending heat all the way down to my core. It made no sense to have this reaction to a voice, and I had to see if it matched his face.

I bit back a groan. It matched. *Good god.* Testosterone and sex just oozed off him in waves. *Delicious* waves. His jet-black hair went well with his soft hazel eyes and tan skin. Lines appeared on the edges around his eyes—a sign he lived a happy life. His jaw was sharp and defined, and his day-old beard didn't hurt either. I grinned and adjusted my position to face him. His gaze moved from my face down to my legs. His nostrils flared twice and awareness burned through me while he continued his perusal back to my mouth.

Ten points to me for shaving and wearing the summer dress. Maybe it was the spark in his eyes that challenged me. *Well, could be my feisty personality.* But instead of going easy on the handsome man, I slowly ran my tongue over my teeth and tilted my head. "I said try again. That line you used is not original. I've heard it an obnoxious amount of times."

He bit down on his bottom lip, doing nothing to hide his amusement. He raised his eyebrows and leaned an inch closer. "Do you find yourself at a bar alone drinking a gentleman's drink often?" He transformed that smirk into a lazy smile that showcased two dimples. The goofy grin clashed with his broad shoulders and intimidating suit and tie but I sure as hell wasn't complaining. Dimples were my kryptonite.

"I prefer to not classify drinks by gender. I drink what I like. We all should do what we like. Life is too short. But to answer your question, yes."

He nodded and didn't ask before sliding onto the bar stool next to me. His cologne teased me, the masculine scent like leather and mint and something…woodsy. I wanted to scoot closer and drag my fingers over his firm pecs, but refrained. I wasn't sure I liked the guy, but my body didn't care. He ordered an Old-Fashioned and winked when he held up his glass. "Clearly, we have great taste in drinks. To the whiskey of the world."

We clinked glasses and he held my gaze throughout the entire sip. His throat moved and desire shot through me. It was such a simple gesture—a man taking a drink. But he did it so much better than all the other men I'd met at bars. He held it up, taking his time smelling the rich liquid, releasing a small moan. His long fingers made the glass seem so much smaller and ideas flew through my head as to what he could do with those hands… I cleared my throat and took another sip.

I didn't have time for commitments of any kind, not with the Silvas car show lasting the next five days, but a fling with a stranger could help with the stress. It had been at least a month since I'd had an orgasm not produced by yours truly, and before I could rationalize my thoughts, my skin tingled in anticipation. I readjusted my legs, crossing the right over the left, and enjoyed his reaction. He followed the motion with his eyes and ran his tongue over his bottom lip, his mouth a little slack. Yeah, I had nice legs and was proud of it. I opened my mouth to speak but he beat me to it.

"You're direct. I appreciate that." He grinned again, the heat in his eyes unmistakable.

"Why waste time on small talk and fake conversations?" I pursed my lips at him and took my time studying every feature on his handsome face. The strong forehead, the slightly crooked nose, the dusting of gray around the temples giving him a beautiful silver fox look… My nipples tightened with need when he leaned closer — not enough to touch me, but enough for the air around us to ripple with tension. I ran a finger down my neck, drawing his attention to the low dip of my dress. He hummed in approval and I swore his cologne got stronger.

"Can I walk you back to your room when we finish our drinks? I know you're independent, but I'd like to offer my help removing your dress."

I smiled, held up my glass and downed the rest of the amber liquid. "How about I walk you back to your room and I help you remove *your* clothes?"

His eyes lit up with delight and he mirrored my action. Not two seconds later, our glasses were empty and I slid off the tall bar stool. He requested our drinks be charged to his room and he put his hand on my lower back to guide me toward the elevator. I was tall for a woman, two inches shy of six feet, but the handsome stranger still had half a foot over me. My limbs trembled at every small gesture. When he dug his fingers into my lower back, I felt it in my toes. He carefully brushed my hair off my shoulder and when the pads of his fingertips touched my skin, electrifying tingles broke out. My body was a puddle of hormones and lust.

"How long are you in town?" His throaty voice sent chills down my back as he pressed his lips against my ear. He had a commanding tone, strong and deep in timbre. I had no doubt he'd have a wildly successful career as a phone sex worker.

"Five more days," I replied when the elevator doors pinged, announcing its arrival. My speech wasn't recognizable with its hoarse tone. I cleared my throat. "You?"

"Same."

The air stilled when the door shut. It was just the two of us in the small hotel elevator, my pulse racing as anticipation built inside me. My panties were soaked and I wanted nothing more than to have my way with the handsome stranger. "What floor should I push?"

"Tenth." He brought his fingers to my neck and eased my long blonde hair off my shoulder. He trailed the delicate skin behind my ears, down my neck and the exposed part of my back. I shivered when he pressed his lips right where my spine met my neck. "Mm. Your skin is beautiful."

He tightened his hold on my hips and pulled my back flush against him, his beard tickling me while he continued kissing tender parts of me. He brought one of his hands around and cupped my breast, pinching my taut nipple. "Braless?"

"It's summer. Too hot to tame them."

"Sexy. I love that." He pressed the tip between his strong fingers and bit down on my ear just as the doors opened. "After you. Third door on the right."

I strutted in front of him, ever so thankful for my long stride, and led us to his room. He didn't rush, and my impatience grew. I was hot, horny and ready. He took his time getting out his key and slid his heated gaze my direction "What's your name?"

"We don't need to do this part, do we?" I tilted my head at the question. There were no misconceptions here. This was a hookup, a way to relieve stress and enjoy a hot night with a stranger. Names weren't necessary.

"I want you screaming my name each time you come. So, yeah. We do need to do this." His rough tone turned me on and my stomach swooped. "I'm Rylan."

"Fern."

His eyes twinkled and he repeated my name. I moaned at hearing it coming from his lips and he finally opened the door. He let me go in first but gave me no time to take in the surroundings. He picked me up, spreading my legs around his waist, and slammed my back into the door. Rough hands went around my hips and he brought his mouth to mine.

God, he kissed like a fucking summer storm. No warning. *Aggressive. Powerful. Magical.* The burn of the whiskey combined between us as we explored each other's mouths. I arched my back when he bit down and sucked on my bottom lip. It gave me a moment to look into his eyes and the intensity there sent another wave of desire through me. It was electric.

Dirty. Animalistic.

I couldn't satisfy my need to have him. I attacked his mouth, trying to taste all of him in that one kiss.

He groaned and brought a hand to my neck. He squeezed the skin where my collarbone met my shoulder and continued down my body until he got to my breasts. Without missing a beat, he brought his mouth down to my chest and pulled the fabric aside. His breathing got heavier with my breasts exposed, the hitch in his breath causing all sorts of sensations in my core. "Gorgeous. Just gorgeous."

He sucked the sensitive nipple into his mouth, swirling his tongue around it. I jumped with pleasure and fisted his hair. "Yes, use your teeth."

He hummed and bit down, mixing the point of pain and pleasure. He repeated the action on my other breast and I bucked against him. "I love your reactions."

I used his break to slide down his body, enjoying his erection bursting to get out of his pants. Size was so *not* an issue. "Lose the clothes, Rylan."

"Yes, ma'am." He smiled and set me on the ground. It was a highly intimate moment between strangers, but I didn't give two shits. My body was alive. I whipped off my dress and removed the thin black panties that were already ruined. I stood there, naked and needy, and admired the curves of his muscles. His pecs were defined, but his abs and arms were just as impressive. "I'm having a hard time focusing with your fine ass watching me, Fern."

"I didn't take you for needy," I goaded him. His eyes changed from light to a darker hue, now almost green, and his arousal grew. Drunk on power, I undid his belt buckle and helped slide his slacks off. His cock sprang free and my core throbbed with need. I desperately wanted to feel all of him inside me, stretching me thin and making me forget my name.

"You're licking your lips looking at my dick. My self-restraint only has so much control." His voice came out huskier and I grinned.

"It's a nice dick. I want to ride it." I reached out and wrapped my fingers around it. I felt his heartbeat in his swollen cock, the head displaying a small bead of moisture. My hand almost covered half of it and I gave him a couple of pumps. He shook at my touch but I didn't get more than ten strokes before he picked me up and tossed me onto the bed. "Woah!"

"You're sexy as hell," he said, his tone exciting me. His face had a predatory smile and I was into it. *Really into it.* He didn't wait for me to respond before kissing and sucking the sensitive skin around my neck and down my ribcage. He brought his fingers to my clit and swirled around it, inserting two fingers inside me. "You're soaked. All for me. Mm."

"Go faster," I said into his neck. The faint scent of sweat mixed with his cologne and it made me drunk. He finger-fucked me to the point I was desperate, seconds away from exploding, but he removed them. "I'm desperate. Don't stop."

"I can't watch you scream my name like this." He slid down the bed so he kneeled on the floor. I thought he was about to go down on me, but he spread my legs apart and used two hands. Ten digits. It was too much. My legs tightened. A burning hot wave of pleasure started in my clit and spread to my limbs. He increased the pressure on my swollen clit and explored the rest of my folds, letting me ride out the wave.

"Rylan, fuck. Yes!" I arched my back and screamed. My legs shook as the orgasm settled down, but he didn't give me any time to recover.

"I can't get enough of your reactions. You're dynamite."

"It's your touch," I replied but grabbed a pillow to muffle my response when he hovered over me and put his teeth down on my nipple. He used one hand to stroke me while giving me the perfect combination of pain and pleasure. He worked me right to the point where the teasing became too much, and I moaned when a second orgasm took control. I yanked his hair and dragged his face to mine, desperate to taste him again.

This kiss was just as aggressive, but there was warmth in his eyes when I glanced at him. Our bodies clung together, the heat building between us until a dull ache began in my core. I wanted all of him. Reading my needy moans, he pressed one last kiss on my lips before getting off the bed. He sheathed himself in a condom from his wallet and gave me a long look. "You're sure?"

A part of me appreciated the gesture, the last question. But my pussy throbbed and I was going to die if he didn't enter me soon. "One thousand percent. Get inside me, Rylan."

His grin was the perfect answer. He held on to my hips and thrust into me in one swift motion. I swore I saw stars. I gripped the sheets around us while he groaned in pleasure. It was intoxicating, knowing he enjoyed it. But the position wasn't doing enough for me. I motioned for him to go to his back and he obeyed.

"God, you're a sight Fern," he breathed. His voice dropped an octave lower, his pupils almost blocking out the green orbs. I slid down onto his cock, releasing a long growl when he stretched me further than I had been in a long while. "*Jesus*, you feel amazing."

I grinned and pushed his hands above his head, pinning them down. I rocked my hips, perfected by years of doing Zumba, and he lost control. He slammed his mouth to mine, our teeth clashing as I rode him. Our bodies blended into one and sweat dripped down my spine. He broke free of my restraint and squeezed my ass.

A third orgasm was close. I could feel it, my stomach muscles clenching when we found our rhythm. He read me like a goddamn book and brought his thumb to my clit. I dug my nails into his firm skin and quickened my pace, leaning forward. The pressure was perfect and I clung to him, screaming his name, riding out the orgasm. He tightened his hold on my hips when he tensed.

"Say my name when you come, Rylan," I commanded with the little voice I still had. His eyes lit up and he obliged. My name left his lips as he did three final thrusts before the sexiest sound came from his mouth. It was a growl and a moan and *fuck* if I didn't want to keep it.

"Christ," he said between pants. "Incredible."

He picked me up like I weighed nothing—and I was a curvy woman—and set me on the bed next to him. He patted my ass and gave me a swift kiss on the shoulder. "Let me clean up. Stay put."

I always appreciated hook-ups where the stranger gave me the needed recovery time. I could catch my breath without worrying about what was next. My body was flushed, my legs shaking from the strong orgasms. I didn't have time to get up before he came out of the bathroom and plopped back on the bed.

"You can stay if you'd like." He leaned on his elbow and my heart lurched. He looked so perfect with his lone curl escaping in the front. I never stayed but I almost thought about it with him. *Almost.*

"Can't. I have a huge event tomorrow. My job may or may not be on the line."

"I have every confidence in you."

"Thanks, handsome." I re-dressed quickly, forgoing my panties. The stress of the event came back despite the three orgasms and I gave Rylan one more glance. "You know…I wouldn't be opposed doing this again while you're in town."

His entire face lit up in a grin and he grabbed a hotel key from his nightstand. "Five more nights here. Come in any time after nine."

"Awful trusting of you, just meeting me," I said, looking at the white key card in my hand. The gesture moved me…it was too trusting. But I couldn't stop the excitement at the thought of seeing him again.

"Sweetheart, I've just been inside you and made you scream my name three times. I'm game if you are, but the ball's in your court." He relaxed into his pillows, his entire body loose and on display.

I licked my lips and gave him another glance. "Then I guess we'll see what happens."

"Can't wait."

Then I left the amazing specimen of a man in the room and went to obsess over the car show that could very well be my last one.

Chapter Two

Rylan

I hated St. Louis. I hated its sport teams, its disgusting humidity and the arch. I mean, what was the point? Sure, it was a symbol of welcoming as the States expanded westward, but it was a metal upside-down *U*. That was it. Chicago was a real city, *home*, and if it wasn't for the fantastic hookup the night before, I would've thought about withdrawing from the show. After all, Silvas were not my thing. Old cars that weren't meant for driving weren't my thing.

Computers *were* my thing, but it didn't matter.

The welcome packet sat on the desk — RYLAN CIRULA in big, bold letters next to the '67 Meridian label. Vaughn Cirula had left this Earth without reaching his goal of earning Gold Accreditation and Original Model Award for his precious Silvas. He had only loved two things his entire life, my mom and his Silvas, and the bitter taste of resentment bubbled inside me. A dull ache began forming behind my eye and I pinched the bridge of my nose to let it pass. My sister Analisa referred to them as *guilt-aches* but I refused to accept her term. They were stress headaches and I knew why.

I had a million-dollar cyber-security business to run with my partner, Flynn Mitchell, and instead of being back in my office, I was stuck in the armpit of the Midwest. *Thank god for Fern.* The feisty blonde was perfect for five days in my own version of hell. She had the body of a goddess, was wild, vocal and on the same page as me. My skin tingled, thinking about her, and I shook my head. Giving her the hotel key card was out of character for me. Our family lawyer had made a hell of a case about protecting our assets—and that meant screening dates, friends and anyone who came into our home. But I was hours away from home and Fern had no idea who I was. I couldn't think of a better situation. *Well, maybe if I weren't at the goddamn Silvas car show for an entire week.*

My phone vibrated, Analisa's name popping up, and I put it on speaker. "What's up, sis?"

"Making sure you haven't jumped ship. You checking in today?" Her voice was too chipper for seven in the morning, but she'd always had too much energy. Even with three young kids, she ran around like she drank six Red Bulls a day.

"I'm about to head there. Did Mom make you call me?" *Yup.* Didn't matter I was a thirty-five-year-old man—my mom still used my younger sister as a middleman. It was easier that way. Analisa called our mom twice a week—I called twice a year. "I'm not backing out. I paid for registration already and it was a bitch getting Rayme here."

"I love how you're using her name now. Dad's stupid nickname finally won you over," she said, an obnoxious snort following. "I'm glad you made it safely. Send pictures when you can. Mom's here for the week with the excuse to help babysit, but we all know she doesn't want to go back to the house."

"She either needs to move closer to you and Rick, or move in with you and Rick," I replied just as the headache came back. I grabbed the bottle of aspirin and popped a couple of pills in my mouth without water. "Anyway, I should head out. I want to walk the place, see how I'm going to unload Rayme in the judging zone. I mean hell, if I come back with a fucking speck of dust on her, Mom will know and write me out of the will."

"Yeah, because that matters to your rich ass." She snorted again and yelled something to one of my nephews. "Look, Peter just had a fart that was questionable. I need to go." She didn't wait for a reply before hanging up, and I made the way down to my SUV. An obnoxiously large trailer sat behind it, my dad's precious Rayme in the back. Driving six hours with that huge thing dragging my back tires down had tested all my patience. I couldn't go over sixty miles an hour and despite not giving a shit about the entire process, worry had consumed every thought the entire drive. *Did I hit a bump too hard? Is Rayme okay?* God, I did *not* need to be worrying a car.

They didn't have names, feelings or any place in the family. Except Vaughn Cirula had loved his car more than his son. *Great. Pity party for one.*

The summer sun already had heat rising from the pavement and I regretted wearing a black shirt the second I walked outside. I pulled the tight material from my chest and hoped to get some air in there, but no luck. I opened the back of the trailer just to make sure the 'Va was okay, and she was fine. No scratches, chips, missing tires or whatever the hell could go wrong.

I hadn't been joking about being cut off from the family if I even left a single scratch on the car. After all, the hardest Accreditation was Original Model — where they judged the Silvas' current condition, comparing it to the state it was in when created in 1967. It was nearly impossible to get, yet here I was, trying because of the *guilt*.

"I don't care, Rebecca. The vendors arrive in two hours and our generators are not here. We paid the invoice. We have confirmation. Make it happen."

The voice caused me to turn and I couldn't stop my grin. Sexy Fern from last night marched from the lobby of the hotel, her blonde hair piled on top of her head and a phone pressed into her ear. "No. Absolutely not. Don't call me until it's fixed and if it's not fixed by nine, you'll be hearing from our lawyer. Is that clear enough? Good."

Her attitude intrigued me. She wasn't afraid to say what was on her mind — calling me out instantly on the lame pickup line — and the take-no-shit tone got me hot. I wouldn't mind her bossing me around in the bedroom that night. I took a couple of steps toward her. But she hadn't seen me yet and her face was set in a determined scowl when she got into her black Chevy.

It was probably better we didn't talk. Morning-afters weren't my favorite thing and she had the key. She could decide all on her own if she wanted a repeat or not. I didn't chase women and, despite how attractive she was and how great we'd been together, I didn't plan to now.

Blasting some Rolling Stones, I pulled out of the lot and drove the twenty minutes to the venue. The middle of a suburb didn't seem like a good place for an event, but I kept the thought to myself. The event itself was spread out across a college campus, but it wasn't a school I had heard of before. *Must be small.* Thank god I'd got there with time to spare because the streets were narrow and there wasn't a lot of space to back in the trailer.

The map I'd gotten in the mail showed six parking lots used for the event, a racetrack for different showcase cars to give rides to patrons, an entire section for the Golden Year 'Vas, and the swap-meet area that consisted of most of the show. I'd read, too, that the town shut down all nearby major roads for a joyride with all the Silvas Clubs across the country. *Who knew there were Silvas Clubs?* I sure as hell hadn't.

The packet also insisted there would be security patrolling the grounds after hours since we were required to leave our Silvas each night—I mean, come on, most of these guys were obsessed with their 'Va—they trusted a security guard to protect it? No way. I had to make sure because, once again, Rayme had more value in the family than I did.

I found the entrance without issue due to the billion signs advertising the show and took note that there weren't any security guards patrolling. That was unacceptable if I was supposed to leave Rayme there for three nights. Great—my headache came back and it wasn't even day one of the event. The two-way lane led farther into the campus and I slowed at a four-way stop. There was a tent set up and a golf cart sitting just beyond the grass.

"Excuse me, can you point me in the direction of Christine Scott's office?" I waved at the first person I found and the young woman widened her eyes at me as a fierce blush crept up her pale neck. I grinned at her reaction. It wasn't unusual for me to get stares, but this girl was young. Either in college or a recent grad. *Not my style.* "Please? I'd really appreciate it."

"Uh, hi. Yeah. Um, head down this main road and turn left at the second stop sign. There are temporary offices set up there but... I don't think people are supposed to be here yet." She bit her lip and gave me a worried glance. "How did you get in?"

"No security up there." I pointed down the road I'd entered. "Will there be guards posted there soon?"

"Damn." She sucked in the side of her cheek and shook her head, looking way too stressed for someone so young. "Fern needs to know about this right now. Excuse me."

Fern? My interest suddenly got way more invested. She began walking away, but I spoke louder. "Fern, you said? Blonde, tall, an attitude?"

"Yeah. That's Ms. Laughlin to a tee." She laughed and gave me a wave. "I need to call her. See you." She walked off with a radio to her mouth and I sped toward the offices. Could my luck really be that fucking good? *Doubtful.* But hope was the devil and a spark of it was enough to have my blood pumping and my gaze scanning for the blonde.

The girl's directions were helpful and accurate so I parked the car with enough room to back the trailer out when I left and eyed my surroundings. A small group of people lined the parking lot, with bottles of spray paint everywhere. Blonde hair stuck out, but I didn't get a chance to see if it was Fern. She was just far enough away for my pulse to pick up, but I was letting last night mess with me. There had to be tons of women named Fern, who had long tan legs and messy blonde hair... *Okay. Shit. It has to be her.*

But I didn't get to find out for certain. A tall, thin woman with large blue eyes and graying red hair appeared next to me. I smiled at her, hiding my annoyance. That was one trait I'd inherited from my dad, laying on the charm when it suited me. "Good morning. Are you Christine Scott?"

"Hi, yes. And you are?" She narrowed her eyes, studying me, but not with malice. It was curiosity...and desire? *Weird.*

"Rylan Cirula. '67 Meridian entered for Gold Accreditation and Original Model, ma'am. It's nice to put a face to a name." I held out my hand. She blushed, her cheeks turning flaming red, and gave me a firm handshake. "I know we can't check in until nine, but I wanted to get here early and take a look around, if that's all right. Lot of family emotions at stake this year."

"Oh, um, of course. I take it your trip here was smooth?" She cleared her throat and kept smoothing down the front of her white polo. The label—*Cruising Silvas* —was on the top right, just beneath her shoulder. The fact that there was an entire world of Silvas aficionados was news to me, but these people were die-hard fans. They held three shows a year all over the nation and this one, Midwest Mileage, was the biggest. Christine and I had spoken a handful of times setting up registration and her voice didn't match her appearance at all. But that didn't matter, and I shook away the errant thought.

"It was a great trip, thank you." I grinned at her again, noting her reaction to me. Her gaze heated for a second before she masked it with professionalism. "Is it okay if I walk around? See how I can back my trailer into the judging area?"

"Yeah. Our workers are here today, getting set up for the vendor check-in tomorrow, but anyone with a yellow or teal shirt should be able to help you. My assistant and I will set up a table for check-in under the white tent in a couple hours. Please make sure you bring the packet with you and we can get you the necessary items."

"Great. Thank you, Christine." I gave her a nod and took off toward the gravel lot where the group of people huddled around. I rubbed the back of my neck as the early morning sun beat into it and I didn't envy the group of six. They bent down, spray-painting the gravel into sections. The bright red paint stood out against the dark pavement and a familiar frame bent low…low enough for small shorts to form around her ass. *Mm. A great ass.*

"Now, Fernie, what in heavens are you bendin' over for? Use the spray gun. You don't need to be hurtin' yourself on day one, honey." An older gentleman hobbled over to Fern and put a hand on her back. "Don't be a hero. Use the spray gun."

"Rich, I'm fine. This is a nice break from dealing with the vendors. I appreciate you looking out for me, but age before beauty. You get the spray gun, I do the grunt work." She elbowed him in the side without real force and they both chuckled like old friends. The gesture pleased me — the camaraderie between them was genuine and I felt intrusive watching them.

"Hey there, sir. How's it going?" The older gentleman, Rich, saw me and gave me a grin that had several missing teeth. "If you're here for the judgin', you ain't in the right spot. Fernie is in charge of operations, Ms. Scott does all the judging."

"I just came from Ms. Scott. I wanted —"

Fern spun around, her warm blue eyes the size of saucers. "What are you—" She stopped, glancing quickly at Rich before she settled herself. "Excuse us,

Rich. I think I'll take him to the offices. Need me to grab you anything?"

"Feel free to find me money, Fernie." Rich didn't wait for a response before walking off to continue spraying the ground with the red paint. That left Fern and me...and I couldn't explain why I was so happy to see her, but my grin stretched across my face and my week didn't seem so goddamn bad as it did before. In fact, something real close to excitement coursed through me.

"I can't believe—"

"Shut up. Come on." She gripped my elbow and maneuvered me to a golf cart about ten yards away. She didn't use enough pressure to hurt me, but her nails definitely dug into me a bit. "Damn you, Rylan."

"Not the reaction I was going for, but I'll take it. Is there a reason you're dragging me away?"

She pointed at the passenger seat in the golf cart and I obeyed her unspoken command and sat down. Fire burned in her eyes and while I lived on the wild side in the business world, something about her expression stopped me from poking the bear. Her nervousness was palpable and, like the mature adult I was, I let her fill the silence.

She started the golf cart and sped down the road, the grounds getting farther away as the seconds stretched into minutes. We were near the entrance—where two guards now stood—before I spoke. "I'm glad there's security now. It worried me when I got here."

"Why are you here?" She stopped the cart near a large yellow and white tent and turned her entire body toward me. Her sleeveless teal shirt clung to every one of the curves I'd explored last night...her toned, tan legs on display. Legs that wrapped perfectly around my waist, clutching me to her. She snapped her fingers. *Shit. She said something.*

"Hm?" I raised an eyebrow and tried giving her a cute smile.

She didn't buy it. "Rylan...stop looking at my legs."

"They are fine legs. Distracting when I know how they feel wrapped around me," I replied, lowering my voice just enough to see her blink three times too fast. I let my gaze move to her ample breasts and enjoyed the light outline of her nipples...despite her pissed-off expression, I could see she felt our attraction. I would sell my company if I was wrong. "So, Fern Laughlin. VP of Operations, I take it?"

She released a long sigh, rubbing her hands on her neck. It wasn't meant to be a sexy gesture, but fucking hell, she let out a small grunt and it took all my willpower not to kiss her. She didn't seem embarrassed or awkward, but genuinely inconvenienced at seeing me. I shouldn't have found joy in that...but I did.

She pressed her lips together and stared at me head-on before saying, "Yes, that's my title, Rylan. Are you registered? Do you have a Silvas and are getting it authenticated?"

"I take it saying yes is not a good thing for you?" I scooted closer so our legs touched, my jeans rubbing against her bare ones. She didn't move away and I ran my finger down her neck, the sensitive skin breaking out in goosebumps. "But yes. I'm registered for Gold and Original Accreditation."

"Shit," she said, pinching the bridge of her nose. "Fuck, man. I can't do this."

"Can't do what?" I lowered my mouth, pressing my lips right beneath her ear. She shivered and my dick woke up at her small moan, just a preview of the sounds I knew she could make. She smelled like suntan lotion and flowers and the craving to taste her again hit me hard. "I really hope you use that card tonight. Last night was—"

"No. I can't fuck someone registered in the show. It's unethical." She put her hands on my shoulder and pushed me away just enough to separate us. She took a long breath, slowly opening her soft blue-gray eyes lined with long dark lashes. She met my gaze, the heat and attraction boiling in them, and gave me a tight smile. "I'm sorry. Last night was amazing. Perfect, actually. But my job is too important. I'll drop you off at the offices, but please…don't…don't act like we know each other. I can't let this affect my career. You need to understand."

She didn't wait for a response before giving me an impatience glance. "Come on, Rylan. I'll say you were a confused owner. We get them all the time. No big deal."

I didn't respond, and the tension around us not enjoyable. An odd sensation formed in my gut. Disappointment? Unacceptance? I wasn't sure, but I knew that I wasn't done with her. Not by a long shot. Feisty Fern with an attitude was my kind of woman, and she needed to accept we were good together for the rest of the week.

Chapter Three

Fern

It wasn't even nine in the morning and I was thinking about putting whiskey in my coffee. No one would even know. If anything, it would calm my nerves and give me some goddamn common sense, because I shouldn't be thinking about taking off my clothes for Rylan. *Again.*

Why does my mysterious hookup have to be entered in the show? Jesus. I grunted and splashed water on my face, collecting my thoughts on how to handle the situation. Andrew Rosales, my boss, had a strict policy on not mixing business with pleasure — and I couldn't afford to do anything where he could let me go. He even made us sign a contract saying we understood the ramifications if we broke the rule. So yeah, taking any chances was off the table. After all, if we didn't increase sales by five percent, I could be fired on Sunday.

Fired. Unemployed.

Yeah—Rylan might've been a sex god in a previous life with those abs and perfect hair…but his body didn't do much good when compared to my job. Career versus a good time. I prided myself on my ethics and snorted at the stupid debacle. Of course, I'd pick my career. It was who I was and what I loved doing. No sexy guy would take that away despite the insane chemistry. We could have polite conversation. That wouldn't be weird and I could still ogle him.

Confident about my resolution, I left the bathroom and ran right into Andrew. His shirt was untucked and his hair a mess, quite different from his normal appearance. In the eight years I'd work there, he'd looked disheveled twice. Once, when there'd been a death in the family and the second, when someone had hit his car. "Hey, boss, how's it going? Everything okay?"

He faltered for a second, pocketing his phone, "Fern, good morning. The layouts going okay?"

Okay, weird response. I rolled with it. "Sure thing. We have four hundred vendors already paid and my guess is we'll have at least fifty walk-ins. I raised registration prices by fifty dollars and it's paid off so far." We'd already made over twenty thousand dollars more than we had last year due to my aggressive marketing plan—calling each vendor one-by-fucking-one and getting them to pledge to come. I was beyond proud of that feat—vendors could be the grumpiest, most foul-mouthed, awful people—but they also could be the best people in the world. It was a fifty-fifty shot. "I'm about to head out and help Rich, Karl and Gary finish lining the swap-meet lots so we can run electricity and get lights set up. You need anything?"

"Good. That's good, good, good." He blinked a lot and the expression on his face gave me an uncomfortable feeling. It was a mixture of worry and...something like pity. "Everything's great."

I headed toward the door, but he said my name again, stopping me. "Yeah?"

"There weren't any signs on the drive here advertising the show and where people need to go for registration. You need to hang them up and make sure this place is accessible. I would've thought they would be up by now." He frowned, crossing his arms and staring me down. Gone was the worry and weird expression he'd had seconds before. He had a little fire to his tone and I fought the urge to roll my eyes.

Of all the years I had been doing this job, he *never* showed up until day two. It was two hours into day one and he had the balls to ridicule me for something I had never messed up? I was damn sure the signs were hung, because I'd done it myself. Plus, Rylan had found everything just fine. I gave Andrew a tight smile that hopefully didn't look too bitchy because he was still in charge of my career and replied, "Open the email I sent you last week. It has a detailed agenda for each day so you can monitor what should be done at what time."

He owns the fucking show. He should know this shit in and out. I sure do.

"Did it?" He raised one eyebrow and that simple gesture was so condescending I dug my fingernails into my palm to prevent a comeback that would ensure I got fired.

Christine Smith—another one of the VPs—walked in and headed straight to Andrew's office without giving me a second of her attention. We worked together ten months of the year and got along for the most part, but a tinge of dread formed in my gut when she didn't say a word to me. Everything was different this year and I had no idea why.

False. I did. But I refused to think it was because they were going to fire me. "Morning, Christine," I attempted a conversation. She liked talking about her kids or her dogs so I went with the first thing I could think of. "Is your daughter coming to help out again this year?"

She slid her gaze to me for a second and gave me a small smile that didn't go near her eyes. It looked out of place on her, as though she'd forgotten how smiles worked. Andrew stiffened next to her, a loud cough coming from him.

Christine replied after thirty seconds of awkward silence. "Hey, Fern. Yeah, she just got here." Then she went into Andrew's makeshift office and shut the door. *Awesome.*

My boss and other VPs were having meetings without me and while it pissed me off, I had a show to run. That was the thing about *car* people. Everyone thought the show would be amazing even if we nixed having the vendors or the swap-meet, but that was how we got people to buy tickets to come in. Why would any sane person buy a ticket to enter a show when all they got to see was rich people's Silvas being judged? The fun stuff, stuff I was in charge of, brought them in and *that* was my priority.

I could deal with them later. The fucking generators were my main focus—the vendors paid ass-loads of money to have a generator available and the company we had a contract with didn't have them on site. No generators meant loss of profit. Kayla Monahan, my assistant for all the events, had the tenacity of a shark but the face of an angel, and I adored her. She busted her ass teaching snotty little third-graders during the school year and helped me with the show two months a year. If there were an MVP award, it would go to her. I radioed to her and she responded within the second.

"Kay, can you help Rich and Karl finish numbering the lots? They have them lined up and marked. We just need to label the spots before vendor check-in tomorrow."

"Sure thing, boss lady. We'll get it done. Have their files been organized by numbers yet?"

"Ah, I don't think so. They were in the back of the blue storage bin out on the northeast tents. I can try and make it out there later."

"We'll do it. Go deal with the latest drama, mama."

I sent a quick prayer of thanks for having found her and called Rebecca back about the generators. It wasn't a fun phone call but an hour later, the generators were en route and wouldn't get in until nine at night. *Mission completed. Next issue – signage.*

Our company had three trailers of supplies that traveled to and from our offices every year for the show and it was Andrew's idea to rent out a row of garages to store everything for the week, which was a great idea…except the people who'd unloaded it had left no trace of organization and it took thirty minutes of searching dark, damp and humid garages to find more signs. I hated that he was even a bit right about putting up more advertisements around the makeshift arena, so it wasn't with dignity when I tossed the rolled-up signs onto the cement. "Signs my ass," I mumbled to myself.

Dripping in sweat, I began loading the thirty signs into the back of the large cargo cart, one by one because they were so large and bulky, when someone cleared their throat. It was guttural and filled with amusement. I knew that deep sound. *Rylan.*

My body didn't give a shit about my ethical issues and I instantly became even hotter. It was like my clit had a radar when orgasms were near, and all my thoughts were controlled by my hormones. *His hands, his mouth, his abs...* I wiped my forehead, fanning myself when sweat pooled between my breasts. "You again."

"It shouldn't be sexy watching someone pick up signs and set them in a cart, but fucking hell, Fern." He entered the garage, bringing with him all his testosterone and cologne. It wasn't fair how good he smelled when I smelled like stale deodorant and sweat. "I'm going to be honest with you. I don't like not getting what I want."

"Tough. The world really isn't fair. Haven't you learned?" I crossed my arms as a barrier, but he stepped closer. Two feet away from me. His gaze heated over, his teeth grazing his bottom lip. I might've moaned a little and I squirmed. "Why are you still here? Those who are getting judged only needed to check in and that takes ten minutes. Cars aren't unloaded until tomorrow."

"I read the packet and understand how it works, but I'm going to be honest. The car is the furthest thing from my mind right now with you standing in front of me looking like you do. Your pulse is racing in your neck, Fern. Your cheeks have a slight blush to them and I bet if I step closer..." He did. "See? You're rubbing your lips together. Why? Is it because you want me just as much as I want you?" He stepped even closer, blurring the lines of professional and personal when he cupped my chin with his large, talented hand. I should've pushed him away. I should've said no. I should've said farewell and walked out of the garage.

I did none of those things. I uncrossed my arms and rubbed my neck. He watched the motion, his gaze trailing to my hardened nipples, then to my mouth. I gulped. The humid air crackled between us when he moved his hand to the back of my neck, bringing his mouth closer to mine. He left an inch between our lips, the anticipation almost too much to bear.

"Just one taste?" he asked, as though one taste would satisfy the burn.

"Like a shot of whiskey." Then I pulled him to me.

Goddamn fireworks. His touch set my body on fire — no more thoughts of what ifs and being unemployed. It was just us in a hot garage in the Midwest summer. I clutched the edge of his shirt, pulling him closer to me so I could kiss him deeper. He groaned. I thrust my tongue farther into his mouth, sucking on his and getting all of his tastes. Heat pooled around my core, my entire body throbbing with desire.

It went on for what seemed like hours, our shared energy and passion distracting me from everything outside. It was just Rylan. He bit down on my bottom lip, sucking it until it stung, and my legs shook — it had never been like this with anyone else in my entire life. And as much as it terrified me, it turned me on and I didn't want to stop.

An engine backfired, the sound rivaling a shot, and we jumped apart like two kids getting caught. His dark hazel eyes were wild, shooting a thrill through me at how much he was affected. My hot stranger looked disheveled and, *damn*, it was cute.

I rubbed my swollen lips, trying to calm my heartbeat, but it increased when Christine's daughter walked by. She hummed to herself, her short summer dress shifting with each step. She smiled when she saw me in the garage, but her gaze flew to Rylan and her entire posture transformed.

"Hey, Fern. Who's this handsome fella?" She puffed out her already large breasts and sauntered up to Rylan. "I'm Marla and I know I haven't seen *you* before."

"Rylan Cirula. Nice to meet you. Do you work here as well?" He gave me one quick glance, his expression clearly saying we weren't done. It thrilled me. He wasn't playing games by flirting with Marla, who was a walking sex-bomb. "I asked about signs because I got lost on the way in, even though I know I'm early. Could you point me in the direction of the sandlot?"

"Hm, what's the sandlot again, Fern?" She twirled her hair in her fingers, her wedding ring glinting in the sunlight.

"Parking for owner trailers. They unload their cars past the alley but park the trailers there. It's in the northeast lot," I replied, hoping my voice didn't shake. We'd almost gotten caught. I wasn't a horny teenager behind the bleachers, despite my actions. *Okay, maybe a little.* I gave Rylan a tight smile. "Hope that helps, Mr. Cirula."

"It did. You were very helpful." He winked, then joined Marla. "Mind walking me up there, Marla?"

She giggled and put her arm through his. "Sure. See you later, Fern!"

They left and while Marla typically annoyed me with all her brazen flirting and extra-marital affairs, I was thankful. I needed the moment to collect myself — again — and hang up the signs. It was tedious, time-consuming, and would surely take my mind off Rylan Cirula.

Three hours later, the signs were all hung up, but new issues took precedence. The truck of golf carts was stuck four states away, our sponsors wanted a larger lot even though we'd met ten times and gone over the specs, and Christine and Andrew had mentioned our lack of ticket sales four times. *The only thing they thought to say to me. Assholes.*

It was a sick cycle. Every year, I took their complaints and second-hand compliments and bottled up my anger. It always came out during the event how rude they could be and it made me question why I did this job. Highs and lows, ups and downs — the rollercoaster of my career was never ending. Tension formed in the lower part of my back and I took two minutes to massage the knots. *Fuck Andrew.* His condescending remarks were out of line — how could he not realize the show wouldn't function without me?

Will people still come if we lost ten judges? Yes.

Will they still come without the joy-ride at the end? Yes, again.

Will they come without the vendors or entertainment sprinkled throughout the three-day show? No. They wouldn't and I was sick of Andrew talking like I was the third wheel of the business. I grunted and took a long swig of water.

My neck burned and I was digging more sunscreen out of my bag when Rich and Karl found me. "Fernie — come with us."

"Is everything okay?" I panicked, wondering what else could go wrong. I already had Kayla organizing the registration packets alphabetically, numbering over four hundred lots and taping down the inside vendor spots. Nothing else could go wrong or I'd get a hernia.

"Shh. Come on." Rich grabbed my elbow and pushed me into his golf cart. I had known him for eight years and I loved him like he was my own grandpa. Most of the time, I loved him more than my nomad parents, who moved from state to state without informing me or my brother. Rich and Karl were a constant in my life and he was about the only person who could boss me around. He was in his seventies and loved Silvas so much he came back to work the show every single year. My chest felt heavy thinking about his health scare a couple months earlier, and I relaxed. He was doing just fine now. We drove five minutes in the golf cart until we hit one of the registration tents. "You need a beer."

"Wait—you sprang me for a drink? I don't have time, Rich."

"Correct, but tough shit. We ain't lettin' you leave until you finish at least two. You're all stressin' and everything will be fine." He patted my shoulder and handed me a Bud. Karl was already seated in a chair, as was Gary. Should we have been drinking? *No.* Was there a ton I still had to do? *Yes.* But, hell, they were my family and I held up my beer in a salute.

"Cheers to year eight, fellas." I fought the urge to cry. They didn't know this could be my last year. The last time the four of us sat together and shot the shit…and I wasn't ready to say goodbye to these guys. I chugged the beer despite the sour taste and came up with a new resolve—we would make a fucking profit or I'd die trying.

* * * *

Day one was almost complete. The grounds were done, signs hung, emergency golf carts on their way…and I just had to wait a couple more hours until the generators got here. Christine left after dinner to get ready for the judges to arrive. I snorted. If I thought vendors were bad, judges were worse and it brought me a little joy to know she'd struggle. I would pick my foul-mouthed hooligans over the hoity-toity assholes. The offices were empty, only a car or two still there. Andrew usually left about seven and I knocked on his door, hoping to go over the pre-event ticket sales. The door swung open, Marla storming out of it with red cheeks.

"Oh, hey, Marla." I gave her a quizzical look, but she brushed me off. "Okay then. Andrew, you got a minute?"

"No, I don't." He too brushed right past me with an unreadable expression on his face. "We'll debrief tomorrow morning. We can go over the plan of attack then." He didn't wait for me to respond before marching out of the door, leaving me even more concerned. I succumbed to the fact I would be alone in the creepy place, but jumped when Andrew burst back in. "I forgot to say, one of the owners asked to work in the spare office next door. Let him know when you leave so he doesn't get locked in."

"Sure," I replied but my gut told me exactly who was in the room. Rylan's massive frame was hard to miss and I'd avoided him an hour ago when he walked around the vendor lot. It was for the best, but I couldn't ignore the zing of excitement knowing it would be just us. I waited until Andrew left for real before heading over to the smaller building where we had Wi-Fi for owners to use. He sat at one of the desks, working on a sleek laptop. He was focused on the screen and didn't hear me come in, which was fine by me. I could gawk at him for hours. His jawline destroyed me...hard angles with the slight brush of a shadow lining it. *How would that feel between my thighs?*

"Keep looking at me like that, Fern, I'm going to take you on this desk," he said without looking up. I should've been embarrassed, but I wasn't. Not with him. Not with our chemistry. I moved to sit on the table a foot away from him and he shut his computer. His eyes burned again, leaving no room for misinterpretation. He reached out and ran his hand down my bare leg, kneading his fingers into my calf. "I didn't realize how much I was into strong legs until I saw yours. It's becoming a problem."

"Yeah?" I giggled and swatted his hand away. "You finished up? My boss wanted me to check in with you. Everyone else left for the night, so I need to lock up when you're done."

"Mm. Are you heading out?" He kept his hand on my leg, slowly bringing it up toward my knee and inner thigh. I wasn't sure of the security camera layout, but I didn't want to chance it. I stood up and ignored the slight fall of his expression.

"I am not. I'm here for another couple of hours." I raised my arms over my head, stretching my tight muscles. I could eat whatever the hell I wanted for the entire week and not gain an ounce—all the physical labor and heat were an instant weight loss. Ice cream and pounds of chocolate waited for me in my hotel room. "We have a delivery that got delayed and won't get here until nine."

"No one else can get it?" He furrowed his eyebrows together and damn, it was the cutest thing on his masculine face. "That's late for you to be here yourself."

"Yeah, well, the night security we hired doesn't start until tomorrow night when the vendors get here. Some of them actually camp out in their trailers the entire time." I shrugged at his concerned expression. "I can take care of myself, Rylan. Been doing this eight years. Been surviving on my own a lot longer."

"I have no doubt." He stood, putting his laptop into a small bag before glancing at me. "Since you have some time, mind giving me a grand tour of the place?"

"Marla didn't give you the entire scoop, throwing in as many pick-up lines as possible?"

"She gave it about five minutes before I bored her. For whatever reason, I'm more into a woman who tries to push me away every time I see her. I must be a fan of challenges."

"You clearly have great taste," I quipped and opened the door to him. "Might as well give you the whole production. Hop on in my ride, sexy."

"God, I love it when you talk dirty." He gave me a panty-dropping smirk that I felt in my toes, and plopped right down in my passenger seat. "I've never been to any of these events before and I'm curious, so let me pick that brain of yours."

Good god, he had a lot of questions. He asked about the set-up, the profit, the anniversary year, the road show — where everyone who signed up drove in a Silvas caravan that drove for thirty miles together — and how the awards ceremony worked. I showed him every inch of the grounds and we were pulling up toward the entrance tent, where one of my signs fell in a gust of wind. The temperature began dropping, the breeze picking up as evening wanted to shift to night. "Shit — hold on, would ya?"

"You're driving, feisty. I am yours to command."

"Is everything you say filled with innuendos?" I laughed and moved to pick up the tri-fold sign. The small bag of sand didn't weigh enough to hold it down. "I've worked with blue-collared people most of my life and, while I love them to death, I'm used to lame innuendos."

"I don't recall you thinking mine were lame. In fact, I think you're enjoying them." He got out of the golf cart and helped me reposition the sign. That was when the first couple of raindrops hit us. "Shit, is it supposed to rain?"

"Summer storms. They can pop up at any time." I looked at the sky just as multiple bolts of lightning burst across it, showcasing the massive clouds rolling in. It was beautiful, the inky colors of the day turning into night, but so ill-timed. "Damn. If it rains, it could erase the plotted parking lots."

"Let's head in then." He gave my shoulder a squeeze, but another sign caught my attention just down the road. "Fern."

"Hold on, gramps. It won't hit us *that* soon." I took off running and went about fifty yards before reaching for a zip tie in my pocket to place, hoping it would help secure the sign back on the fence. If I had to rank signs by their importance, this was the top dog. It told owners, judges, vendors or customers where to go as soon as they entered the event premises, and if we lost the sign...I'd get bitched at by Andrew. I struggled with putting it back up, because each time I placed one corner, the wind got it.

"Here, I'll help." Rylan joined me and his focused expression warmed me. "Hurry up with the ties—the rain is going to start soon."

"Thanks," I put the plastic in my mouth and, with four hands, we got the sign balanced. I secured my two corners, then moved to Rylan's end and did the same. He made no effort to move out of the way and my left shoulder connected with his strong pecs when the first drops hit. "Aw, man. You're going to get wet."

He growled. "I don't mind being wet with you."

"Jesus, always an innuendo," I joked and motioned us to walk back to the golf cart. Each step seemed to cause the rain to fall harder.

"We need to get inside. Where's the nearest structure?" He valiantly tried to shield me from the rain, but it was pointless. It came down in sheets, the temperature dropping by the minute. "Come on, let's run to the tent and check the radar. We could just wait it out."

He shouldered his bag and took my hand. The entrance tent was only a twenty-second sprint away and when we entered it, only a table and chair met us. Rain was the worst thing to happen before vendor check-in and registration. It would wash away the paint and numbers my team had spent six hours doing. It would cause mud everywhere and mud meant less foot traffic. And that meant fewer sales. I groaned, trying not to let the stress take over. "For fuck's sake, why does it always rain?"

"I don't know...but your shirt is soaking wet and, Fern, I'm a sensible man. I've been looking at you and I want to respect your wishes...but fuck, I can't get your body out of my mind." His deep voice hit me in my core and the answer seemed easy. *Sex.* Dirty, wet, orgasm-inducing sex was the perfect distraction from the job. A momentary bliss from everything that was going wrong.

Signs. Andrew. Christine. Generators. Sales. Bullshit.

I needed a huge distraction and as far as distractions went...Rylan was the best.

"Then I guess we should do something about it, huh?"

Chapter Four

Rylan

My dick throbbed, all the blood I had going straight to it. My muscles tightened and I was tense as shit. The teasing from early morning until now had been a test of my restraint because goddamn…I had never been drawn to a woman like I was to Fern. Her answer was fucking important, but I needed it spelled out. "You're going to have to explain yourself, clearly. What is the something we should be doing?"

She giggled, pulled the end of her shirt and lifted it over her head. The rain had soaked her lacy pink bra, her dusty pink nipples bursting to get out of the mesh material. She ran her fingers over their outline, pinching the beaded points. I jerked in desperation. *Fucking Christ.* "Is this not clear, Rylan? Or do I need to spell it out for you?"

I think I grunted—I wasn't sure. But she got a wicked glint in her eye and slowly slid down one of her bra straps, taking her time tracing her fingers over her wet skin. She removed the other strap, letting the bra fall to the ground, and went to the table. Her skin glistened with the rain and it was about the hottest thing I had ever seen. "Rylan. I want you to suck and bite me, please."

I jumped toward her, my need so desperate it should've startled me. I took her sweet, lush breast into my mouth and sucked. Sweat combined with the rain made for an exotic taste, and I swirled the peaked tip in my mouth. She moaned, pulling on the end of my hair to the point my scalp stung. I didn't give a flying fuck about the pain—her sounds were driving me wild. I pinched her other nipple, her back arching when I pulled on it. Thunder roared around us, but her moans were louder.

"*Yes, god.* This. This is what I—" She stopped. I shoved her onto the table so she was on her back and I stood over her near her head. It gave me access to her entire chest and mouth. I bit the base of her neck, right along her collarbone. She tasted like fucking heaven. "*Fuck, yes.*"

"Your body kills me, Fern," I grunted and trailed my fingers down her warm, wet skin. Goosebumps broke out all over her and an idea struck me. "Trust me, okay?"

"Keep touching me like that, you can do what you want."

I grinned at her response. I loved her answer. I grabbed her shirt and tied it around her eyes—leaving her nose and mouth exposed. She shivered, her body heaving with each breath. Something about her racing pulse had my eye twitching and I needed to touch all of her. "I want you to feel everything. Just relax. Can you do that for me?"

Jaqueline Snowe

"I'm so turned on it's only going to take three flicks down there for me to fucking explode." Her throaty voice sent a shiver of craving through me — my pants were so goddamn tight against my cock, I was surprised it didn't burst.

"Mm, I would pay to see if that's true." I traced the outline of her lips with my tongue, enjoying how she shook with need. I teased her relentlessly, so when I bit down on her lip, she screamed. "Three flicks, hm?"

She couldn't answer, she just squirmed. I moved around the table, not taking my hands off her while I unbuttoned her shorts and slid them down her toned legs. Her bare pussy was on display for me and I shuddered. *Jesus. Christ.* She was perfect. Her swollen lips greeted me when I brought my right hand down to her clit but didn't touch it. I spent time on every part except where she wanted it and slid two fingers inside her. "Rock against my hand, Fern."

She obeyed, slowly bringing her hips forward while she took my fingers deeper. My cock was dripping wet at this point, but I didn't give a shit. I sped up my pace and brought my other hand to her clit. "Three flicks, are you ready?"

"*Please.*"

One flick. She bucked against me.

Second flick. She arched her back and tightened her legs muscles.

Third flick — I bent down and sucked her into my mouth for five seconds, gently bringing my teeth around her engorged clit. She exploded. Her legs shook, her entire body convulsing on the table, and I couldn't recall a sexier scene in my entire life.

"*Rylan*, oh my god — shit!" She cried my name three more times, her exposed body turning limp as she rode the orgasm out. "That was more intense than last night."

"Good. You weren't kidding about three flicks, feisty." I kissed her again, allowing her to taste her own arousal from my mouth, and deepened the kiss. She let me push her head back, opening up her throat for me. I grazed it with my tongue until she panted again. "Fern, those sounds will kill me."

"Your mouth will kill me, Ry."

She called me Ry. Pressure built around my heart, nostalgia hitting me instantly with that name. I hadn't heard anyone call me that since— "I don't mean to be bossy, but I need your mouth on my pussy again."

I didn't take another second. I positioned myself before her legs, pushing them as far apart as I could, and admired the view. She had a beautiful pussy and evidence from her first orgasm dripped down her folds...and dear God, I wanted more. I licked it up, swirling my tongue around and while it took more than three flicks, it didn't take long.

Two fingers inside her, my tongue flicking her clit, a little combination of my teeth and she fell apart again. Her guttural moan got my dick even harder and I wasn't sure how much longer I could take it. "Fuck, Fern. You're a goddamn goddess."

She hummed in response and I wiped my mouth on the back of my hand. "Do I get a turn to play, too?" She reached out, pulling my shirt so I pressed against her. "I'm floating right now, but I'm an equal opportunist."

"I like how you think," I replied before untying her shirt from her head. Her wide blue eyes were dark, her pupils dilated with pleasure. She sat up with all the confidence in the world. It pleased me. She shouldn't show an ounce of embarrassment—she was the right combination of curves, warmth and life. She hopped onto the bare grass and eyed me up and down. "What are you doing?"

"Thinking about how good you look under your clothes. Take off your shirt, Rylan." She laughed, the sound coming from deep in her chest. She brought her small hands to my shirt, pressing her naked body up against me while she tried to take off my clothes. I was too tall for her to reach and I helped her out. I was a nice guy like that. She ran her fingers down my pecs, rubbing my muscles as her eyes heated. "Get on the table, Rylan."

"It won't support me."

"If it breaks, it breaks. Get on the table," she commanded and gave me a slight push. She raised her eyebrows and suddenly, I didn't mind doing a single thing she said. "Good. Trust me, okay?"

I tried to laugh, but she didn't wait for a response before covering my eyes with my shirt. She leaned over, pressing her tits in my face and I sucked one into my mouth. "Mm."

"You're a boob guy, aren't you?"

"Your boobs, yeah," I replied, but about jumped off the table when she bit the spot right below my belly button. *How did she even get there that fast? Fuck.* She dragged her tongue around it, kneading my skin with her hands as she went lower and lower. "*Fern.*"

"If you can talk, I'm not doing a good job, am I?" Then she undid my belt and removed all my clothing. It was just us, our sweat-covered skin and our sounds. Best combination ever. Thunder struck, the sound fucking loud, and Fern froze with her mouth barely touching my dick. I wanted to arch my hips forward, just enough to urge her lips, but it took all my willpower to be respectful.

"You—you okay?" *God, my voice sounds like a crazy person's.*

"Oh, yeah...your cock just distracted me." She cupped my balls with her hand, her mouth finally closing around my swollen head. Pure pleasure ripped through me. The ripples shot from my cock, up my spine and all the way around my body. I shuddered. She quickened the pace, my dick touching the back of her throat with each thrust of her mouth and the white-hot desire hit me. It went on forever, time not making sense as she found her rhythm.

"Fern—I'm going to—"

She didn't stop. She went faster, pulling on my balls, and I exploded in her mouth. I reached for something, anything, and came up empty so I gripped the edge of the table, getting all sorts of splinters. "*Fern, god.*"

I bucked against her, riding out the final wave of pleasure. My ears rang, my pulse pounding as though my heart was trying to escape my ribcage. I needed her to understand how fucking good it was. It was just...different. *Better. Hot.* So unlike the countless times I had gotten a blowjob. "Come here."

"Do you have a condom?" She carefully removed the shirt from my eyes and stood over me, not unlike how I sat in the chair at the dentist. *Great—now I'm going to get a hard-on at the dentist.* "I know we aren't teenagers, but I'm impressed if you're good to go already for round two."

"I need at least an hour." I pulled her to me so our naked bodies meshed together. "I'm going to be honest with you, Ms. Laughlin."

She scrunched her nose, a quizzical expression on her face. "Okay, Rylan Cirula."

"Two times with you isn't going to be enough for me." I rubbed her back, already thinking of the ways I could help get the knots out. She had to be tense as hell. "My body is fucking humming right now. That doesn't happen and I'd like to enjoy it as often as I can."

"You know the right things to say to a lady," she replied with an underlying tone I couldn't read.

"That wasn't a line, if you're thinking it is." I pressed my lips to her shoulder, her neck, and tipped her chin up to look at me. "We have four more days together before we go our separate ways. We're both married to our jobs. I say, we enjoy the hell out of each other for the week."

"Nothing personal? Just sex?"

"Psh, *just* sex? How about fucking amazing sex as often and as much as possible?" I wiggled my eyebrows at her a couple of times before she relaxed and laughed. "I can safely guarantee three orgasms a day. If not, you can file a complaint."

"I'll need to get this in writing." She ran her tongue over her bottom lip, amusement swirling in her eyes. Without an ounce of makeup, she entranced me with her beauty. The slight sunburn on her face brought out freckles and *for fuck's sake*, I was a grown man thinking about her freckles.

"You in or no?" I pushed a strand of her soaking-wet hair behind her ear and nipped at her neck. She let out a sound that was a combination of a moan and laugh and she nodded. "Say, *yes, Rylan. I agree to fuck your brains out all week and stay in your hotel room naked.*"

"Yes, Rylan, I agree to let you fuck my brains out all week, provide at least four orgasms a day, and help me forget my name." She stuck out her hand, showcasing her small dimples with a wicked grin. We shook on it, but she pulled me closer to her so our mouths were inches apart. "But two caveats. You pretend you don't know me here and nothing more than a fling."

"Done and done." I kissed her, quick enough to not get excited again but enough to send a message. "Now, let's get these goddamn generators organized so I can get you naked again in my bed. As much as I enjoyed our tent fun, I'd really like to be inside you."

"I like how you think," she said with a smirk. She handed me my clothes but stopped and held up her hand. "In fact, you owe me."

"What's that?"

"Two more orgasms. We shook on four." She shrugged before winking at me. And by god, sex-vixen Fern was hard enough to handle, but playful Fern? *I'm screwed.*

Chapter Five

Fern

Heat. So much heat. And cologne? I stretched in the hotel bed and tensed when someone next to me moved. *Rylan.* I grinned at the sore parts of my body. Every one of my muscles had gotten worked last night and it was well worth it. As much as I craved to stay in bed and wrap myself around his body, I had to get ready for vendor check-in. *My hell on earth.*

"It's four-thirty. Why are you up?" His sleep-filled voice startled me. I thought I'd been quiet enough to not stir him.

"Shit, I didn't mean to wake you." I slid out of bed, but he grabbed my wrist and yanked me back. It wasn't hard, and while I didn't mind being pressed against him, I hadn't expected it. "Hey now!"

"You sure you can't stay longer?" His drowsy voice and warmth were so goddamn inviting. It was even more difficult to leave when he positioned himself over me, nuzzling his face into my neck. His beard tickled my sensitive skin and I shivered. "Stay with me."

"I have to check the maps, make sure the lots are still lined after the storm, and the signs and the—"

"Shh. Too much talking, not enough sleeping." He kissed me, morning breath be damned, and slid his tongue into my mouth. It was a sweet kiss, just enough to get my juices flowing, but not enough to have me say to hell with my job. "I like you here. Naked. In my bed."

"I'll be back tonight, Ry." My voice remained even despite the problematic thoughts running through my caffeine-less brain. *Why do I want to stay? Why is my heart racing? Why is his voice perfect?*

He tensed at the name, but it was so quick I dismissed it. "You bet your ass you'll be back here tonight." He slid down my body, pressing his lips against my neck, collarbone and stomach before lifting his face toward me. Just enough light came from the lamp and his warm, almost tender expression had my breath catching in my throat. "You gotta shower, don't you?"

I frowned while desire continued to pool between my legs. "Um, yes?"

"Good. That solves it." He got up, his extremely massive morning wood greeting me in the dim lightning. "Come on, Fern."

"What are we—what?" I didn't understand his train of thought and wiped the sleep from under my eyes. "I really need to—" Lips met mine, shutting me up. Then he lifted me. A part of me, for just a second, felt safe in his arms. I wanted to snuggle up in them and have him protect me for just a day. But I dismissed the absurd thought.

"I told you I'm a gentleman. I'm going to help you shower." He flipped on the bathroom light and when the it hit his face, my face felt warm. He had the cutest expression. His forehead wrinkled, evidence of sleep still present, and his damn smile…it was a lethal combination. "Get the water the temperature you like."

"I don't have time for a quickie," I snapped. I didn't like my irrational thoughts about how cute he was. I had shit to do.

"Did I ask for one?" He gave me a smug grin and squeezed my ass. "Maybe I just want to enjoy the little time I have with you."

Oh.

He smirked and pushed me toward the small shower. "Plus, I want any chance I can to look at your fantastic tits. That's my real motivation."

"Well, get your fill, Ry." I stepped into the shower, turned on the hot water and my clit swelled when he stepped in behind me. He found my nipples with his fingers, using one hand to grab soap and rubbing it over me. I moaned, enjoying the pleasure rippling through my body. I'd never been into morning sexy time, but hell…I would be now. "I think they're clean."

"I'm just being safe." He continued rubbing and caressing them. Then he slid his hands down my body, making sure all my parts were clean before grabbing the shampoo. He washed my hair and, for the damnedest reason, it was more intimate than everything else we had done. "Your body is amazing but so tense. I hope this is relaxing for you."

I shut my eyes. His voice was too sweet. "Yeah, it is. Thanks," I barked out.

"You're welcome," he replied, his voice dripping with hidden meaning. He massaged my scalp, the sensations giving me shivers all down my body. I turned to mush and he chuckled when I leaned completely into him. "I like making you feel good."

"God, you're so great with words."

"Just being honest." He rinsed my hair and the urge to take him right there overwhelmed me. He was sweet, sexy and *mine*. For four more days. "Woah, what were you just thinking, Fern? Your eyes went dark and I gotta say, it was hot."

"My job is getting in the way of what I'd like to do with you the next four days." I ran my hand down his body, grasping his massive wood before slipping out of the shower. "Trust me, I'd rather spend my day with your cock in every part of me, but I need to go."

"Fuck," he said in a strangled voice. "Thanks for that."

"Think of me if you need to yank one out real quick," I fired back and was met with a devilish grin. "Thanks for the shower. It was great."

"This is just great. I'm hard as shit, wanting you more than my next breath. But fine, go be a badass and run the show." He pinched the bridge of his nose and the gesture sent a thrill through me.

"Will do." I leaned back in the shower and pressed a kiss on his cheek before dressing and leaving him in the room. While the stress had done a number on my sleeping pattern, Rylan had counteracted it and I felt rejuvenated. *Happy. Relaxed.* It was rare and I enjoyed the entire drive to the stadium. Four days of pleasure. It was the perfect recipe for me—I could work, fuck, enjoy orgasms and sleep next to a hunk of a man. Then we would go our separate ways and I could either figure out how to get a new job, or continue the one I loved. It was the best-case scenario.

But the pleasant thoughts shifted when I pulled into the main entrance. My to-do list was longer than the fucking dictionary and reality hit me.

Two hours and four cups of coffee later, I was ready to go. Security were in their assigned locations. Operations staff were in positions. Christine and her judges and owners were separate from my end of the show—thank god—and the generators were in place. We just had to survive vendor check-in, and I could enjoy two glasses of whiskey. I glanced at my watch...barely seven in the morning and my feet already ached.

"You ready, Fernie? Today's our hell day." Rich hobbled into the makeshift office and gave me one of his signature grins.

"I know, Rich. Shit. I'm as ready as I can be. You, Gary and Karl good to go on the south lots?" Four lots, four hundred vendors. We had more signed up this year than any year before and almost eighty percent of them had already paid. This was huge. *And surely a way to get more revenue.* My left eye twitched and I coughed to try and cover it.

"Ten-four. Kayla has the west and Emma has the east. Ruth Anne just got to the entrance tent with all the files. She'll need you there to help start, but it's showtime." He grinned his toothless smile and I took a calming breath. "This is the fun part. Enjoy the ride. When you get to my age, you'll learn there's often not a lot worth stressin' about. You're healthy, it's a beautiful day and we're going to be surrounded by fine-looking Silvas."

"I love when you put things into perspective, Rich. But I would expect that from a living fossil."

He cackled, drawing stares from the rest of the workers, and put his hands on his knees. "You're my favorite, Fernie. Just remember that."

I grinned and got into battle stance, but I was interrupted by Andrew. He stormed into the office area with a livid expression, and my stomach dropped. "What's going on, Andrew?"

"Everything is *just* fine." He spat his words like a bad-tasting food and it took all my power not to recoil because it seemed like that anger was all on me.

"You sure?" His tone didn't match his words—his passive-aggressive leadership style was my least favorite thing about him.

"Pre-show tickets are down. We didn't have enough owners register and I hoped we'd have at least twenty walk-ups, but *nada*. Sales aren't looking good, Fern."

"Almost all vendors paid already. This is huge. Don't discredit that," I fired back and crossed my arms. "The show hasn't even started and it's not forecast to rain. I spent less on marketing than last year and numbers are up. It's a little premature to say we're down in profit, Andrew."

He didn't reply but gave me a long look before going into his office and shutting the door. Andrew was weird to work for and often let us do our own thing. I used to find it empowering, but now…it was lazy. He demanded almost unrealistic expectations from Christine, Gary and me, and he didn't help at all. We each had our own departments and brought our own strengths. Like the fact I'd brought in more money with vendors this year than ever before…or how I had tickets on sale almost a year in advance rather than just a week. I rubbed my temples, collecting my thoughts, and the door opened. Marla, Christine's daughter, walked in dressed in tight yellow clothing. "Hey, Marla."

"Hi, Fern. Good morning to you! Great day, huh?" She gave me an awkward smile, but I couldn't decipher why it was awkward. It was a gut feeling…maybe it was the tilt of her head or the way her gaze slid right past me and to Andrew's door. Or maybe I needed more caffeine.

"Yeah, fingers crossed." I took another sip of the shitty coffee and frowned when she went to Andrew's office. It wasn't unusual for them to work together, but Marla had been reassigned from judging to photography so she could help with marketing. And I had yet to see her take a damn picture.

And he'll blame me for it. I shook my head and refused to think about him. I had a show to run and, by god, I was good at my job. After refilling my portable mug, I stormed back onto the field to check in with Kayla and about ran into Rylan. He stood just outside the tinted door with his hand reaching toward the handle. I could've just taken one more step and have that hand right where I wanted it, but I couldn't. *Damn job.* "Excuse me, sir. Apologies. I didn't see you there."

"Ms. Laughlin. Good to see you. How are you doing?" He ran his tongue over his bottom lip, his eyes dancing with amusement. It was hard not to smile — hours ago I'd left him with a raging boner, dripping wet in the shower. My body warmed up at the memory. "Is everything going smooth with the check-in?"

"Of course, Mr. Cirula. Thanks for asking," I replied and winked. "No issues so far."

"I bet you're great at solving *hard* problems that come your way." He lowered his voice and dropped his gaze to my mouth. It made no sense, to feel his gaze everywhere. But I did. We stood in the middle of sunlight, people busying all around us, and I was drawn to him. His energy, his smile, his *talents*. But the door to Andrew's office flew open, Christine *and* Marla coming out. I'd had no idea Christine was already in there and this made a second time my colleagues had met without me. Anger quickly flared and disappeared in my chest. Another issue to deal with at another time.

"Mr. Cirula, good to see you again. I take it everything went well with getting your '67 here?" Christine gussied right on up to him, sticking her large breasts out a little too much. *Like mother, like daughter.* I fought a laugh at the clear discomfort on Rylan's face. He gave her a tight smile walking past me, but made sure to squeeze my wrist before heading her way. It was a simple gesture, sweet even. I shook my head and geared up to face the heat.

Marla caught up with me and let out a long whistle. While I had no beef with her, the fact she kept meeting with my boss annoyed me. "Yes, Marla?"

"I did some research and Rylan Cirula is the Mr. Moneybags. From the magazine? He's fine as hell, owns his own cyber security company and he's not even forty. Fine. Piece. Of. Man." She fanned herself and took out a stick of red lipstick from her yellow dress. I wasn't sure how, but the skin-tight outfit had pockets. She reapplied her color and smirked at me. "I know I'm married, but if he gave me a second glance, I'd say to hell with Mark."

I frowned, not sure how to respond to any of her comments. I hated infidelity, but it wasn't my business. I would just never talk about it so freely. Also, *Mr. Moneybags*? "How did you—why do you know this?"

"Mom was going on about this young hot-shot owner with a sick car. Recognized the name from the blogs I follow. He's this tech guru in Chicago. Got called Mr. Moneybags online and it stuck with him. His net worth is like some crazy millions and shit. Makes you wonder how many women try to have a kid to get the money. I know I'd try. I mean come on, child support would be amazing from someone like him."

An unfamiliar feeling took hold in my throat—unease? Dread? I didn't like it one bit and Marla took my silence for her to continue talking. "I also heard his dad just died and this—"

"I gotta head out. Kayla just texted me. See you later, Marla!" I jogged toward my golf cart, speeding to get away from her. This was too much...too personal, too invasive. I didn't care about any of that stuff besides the orgasms I'd been promised. His name was Rylan Cirula and he was amazing in bed. He said and did the right things and my body really liked his body. That was all we'd agreed on.

Right?

Chapter Six

Rylan

I had never before seen a grown man bent on one knee with a delicate hand-towel screaming at other full-grown men around him to be precious with their strokes. But now I could mark it off the list of things I'd seen. It was a bit like a shitty comedy movie where I couldn't stop watching even though I hated what I was observing.

Leaning against the brick wall provided me some shade—not enough, but it helped cool me off as the temperatures were already nearing three digits. It just happened to be right where the majority of the Silvas owners were unloading their cars and, goddamn, it was a show. The man I dubbed Beefstick—because of his long beefy arms and skinny legs—wore two fanny packs and held a small toothbrush as he scrubbed the rims around the tires with it. A stab of guilt crept in, making it difficult to breathe at a brief memory of my dad trying to get me involved with cars. I'd blown him off every time, preferring to play with computers or videogames. What an odd time to get a wave of guilt when Beefstick was bent low, his ass crack hanging out, and patting the car's hood like a young child. But guilt didn't pick the best times to resurface. I knew that.

It'd always mattered to my father that I didn't care about what I drove. He'd never said it to explicitly, but he implied it enough over the years, not helping the growing animosity between us. I cared about coding, hacking systems and building shit with my nerdy friends. Analisa was the tomboy and played all the sports, I did the tech thing and he never approved. Sure, our mom said he just didn't understand me, but that didn't matter. Any young teenager wanted the approval of his father.

Even when I made my first million, he just shrugged and mumbled something incoherent about computers taking over the world. While my melancholic mood had its place, here, in the middle of the day surrounded by men and women and their Silvas, was not it. I shook off the memory and did my best to not look like I was an outsider. But it didn't matter. I was.

Not a minute later, Christine approached me with one of her coy smiles and I plastered on my friendly one. The one I used for press releases from our company, the same one I'd also used for the ridiculous magazine shoot where they'd given me the nickname Moneybags. While the experience had been entertaining, it had brought me some unwarranted attention that I didn't have time for…like gold-digging women. "What can I do for you, Christine?"

"Oh, nothing, Mr. Cirula. Just checking to make sure everything is going well. Is your car unloaded already?" She shielded her eyes from the sun despite her sunglasses hanging on the deep cut of her shirt.

"Nope. I'm scheduled at ten minutes before six tomorrow morning, which...why so early?" I'd thought it was a typo the first time I read it.

"Because people start arriving at eight and our noodlers get here to beat the heat and the crowds." She pushed her hair behind her ears and gave me a funny look—like I should've known the answer to my question. I didn't like feeling inferior for *any* reason.

"Uh...noodlers?" My mind went to pasta...and nude people. But neither made sense. "Is that what you said?"

She laughed and put her manicured hands on my forearm. I tensed at her touch, but she didn't notice and kept it there. Some people liked being touched, others didn't. I got it, but unless there was a bond there, I preferred to remain in my bubble. Christine didn't care about that though. Not at all. "Our parking team works for Gary Cho and they use pool noodles to place where the cars should be parked. It provides a soft enough barrier to mark where the Silvas go. You'll see tomorrow. It'll be a hoot."

"Can't wait," I deadpanned.

She squeezed my arm, my sarcasm completely lost on her. "Everyone's been talking about you, Mr. Cirula. You're quite the celebrity here," she said, her pitch a little too high for my liking. She had a wandering and penetrating gaze, as though she was trying to see what was underneath my clothes. I wasn't a fan. "You're going to have the women flocking to you. Between you and me...most of the owners are old folks. You...well, you're not. You're quite attractive, Mr. Cirula."

"I guess I'll have to stay under the radar then." I slid out of her grip and gave her another forced smile. "See you around, Christine."

"Yes, you will! Bye, Mr. Cirula!" She gave me a wide, almost frightening smile and I took off toward the indoor vendor area — the tented structure about as far away from the registration field as possible. It was massive, tape lining the floor with numbers labeling each section alphabetically. The air-conditioning hit me as soon as the doors opened and relief flooded through me. I worked inside twelve hours a day, so this nonsense heat was almost unbearable.

Vans, trucks, trailers…shit was everywhere. It was like college dorm move-in day times a million. There was a sea of people bustling around with wagons and carts, mumbling to themselves and yelling orders at those around them. An older woman carried an entire car full of dolls while another woman held about fifteen clocks in her arms. I didn't understand — this shit looked like a garage sale on steroids. *People pay to come buy this stuff?*

I didn't understand people much, but the air felt nice and it gave me an escape from all the Silvas, and I couldn't say it wasn't entertaining. It had taken me about thirty minutes to walk the length when one person caught my eye. Fern stood in the center of the arena with a radio up to her gorgeous mouth, a clipboard in her hand and her hair up in a messy bob. My mood brightened instantly and I carefully found a path over to her. It was a challenge avoiding the wires, car parts and random shit people sold.

"Ms. Laughlin? There's an issue with a tent that needs your help," I said.

She snapped her gaze to mine and for a second, there was panic. Then she grinned, glanced to my crotch and slowly brought her heated gaze up to my face. "I'm not responsible for a tent in your pants, handsome. Try again."

It felt as though a fist had reached in and squeezed my heart. Her confidence had captured me that first night, how she'd held herself at the bar with her long legs and straight posture, and it was no different now. She commanded attention and she had all mine. Plus, her mind and wit got to me. *Intelligent women are sexy.* "I might need a pipe checked before it leaks. I didn't pay for insurance on it. Any thoughts?"

"Better, but subpar as far as pick-up lines," she replied to me, but then held up her finger and spoke into the radio. "Kayla, do you copy?"

"I'm here, Big Cheese. What's up?"

She smirked and rolled her eyes when I made a face at her nickname. It was adorable and yet so fitting. "How's the situation at K233?"

"As smooth as a dumpster fire. Feel like stopping by?"

"En route." She clipped the black device back on her belt and gave me a resigned smile. "Sorry about your pipe issue. I would refer you to someone else...but I'm not a fan of sharing services." She patted my shoulder and didn't wait for me to respond before walking toward an extra-large golf cart. She didn't get too far before three more venders approached her shouting demands and complaints. She answered each one of them as they fired question after question, some of them yelling and raising their voices. One argued they'd been shorted two inches of their space, another demanded to be moved next to their friend, and the third, well, I had move closer to make sure I heard it right.

He insisted on smoking and wouldn't move outside. Fern put a stop to that one real quick with one call on the radio to security. The older gentleman waddled away, cursing under his breath, and she gave me an amused smile. "Dream job. I know."

I chuckled and let her lead the way out, taking the extra minute to admire her shapely calves and how her shorts hugged her curves in the perfect way. She had a rollercoaster of a body and, goddamn, I almost got hard when she put another slimy guy in his place. Not my best moment, getting turned on when she was just doing her job. Then she looked at me over her shoulder with the coyest expression. "Mr. Cirula, would you like to accompany me and I can drop you back off at *your* area of the event?"

"Of course, Ms. Laughlin. I'd love a ride with you."

We got into her golf cart, her sweet scent of sunshine and sunscreen drifting my way, and I started counting down the minutes until I could have her again. "What time are you expected to leave tonight?"

"Nine. Security is here and fuck, I need a Glendronach 18 on the rocks." She pushed her sunglasses up on her head and stopped the golf cart at one of the corners. "I'm getting hangry. You up for a snack or are you needed elsewhere?"

"I'm yours to command, Big Cheese." We shared a smile and the urge to kiss her caught me off guard. Instead of acting on it, per her rules, I cleared my throat and asked about her whiskey reference. "The first night I saw you drinking that whiskey, I knew you'd be cool and sophisticated. But Glendronach 18? You gotta tell me how you got into it."

"I'm a whiskey woman, *Moneybags*." She started the golf cart and the nickname felt like a punch to the gut. She knew. She knew about my— "Full disclosure, I don't give a shit about your wealth. I don't care what you do...as long as you continue to *do* me real nice. So wipe that worried expression off your face."

Perfect answer. "Pull over."

"Excuse me?" A line formed between her strong eyebrows and she pursed those pink lips with her response.

"Find a tent, or I'm going to kiss the hell out of you right fucking now." I gripped her knee and slowly slid my hand up her thigh. "I'm not joking, Fern. You know your whiskey, you let your employees call you Big Cheese and you just said the best thing I've heard in a while. I know what you taste like and you're really testing my control."

She hummed in response and veered off to a yellow and white tent that was a football field away from the event. Her chest heaved as the golf cart seemed to go at the rate of a fucking turtle. "This is for the part-time help that starts tomorrow. Should be empty."

"Probably best for what I plan to do with you." I slid my fingers farther up her thighs, teasing the edge of her shorts and enjoying her panting breaths.

"Good God, you get me wet with your words." She gulped and pressed her foot harder onto the pedal.

The second we entered the abandoned tent, I attacked her mouth and pulled her onto my lap. She ground against my cock, her guttural sounds getting me hard as fuck. I slipped my fingers up her shorts and found she was telling the truth. She was soaked and I wanted to give her pleasure—anything to let her know how her words made me feel.

My world was filled with money-seeking people. Everyone wanted a piece of it, yet she just wanted me for sex. And I believed her. "You're so sexy, Fern. Goddamn it."

"Right back at ya, handsome. I'm breaking all my rules with you." She sucked my bottom lip into her mouth, holding eye contact with me, and an odd feeling formed in the pit of my stomach. It was stronger than lust...but I wasn't sure what it was. "Tonight, I want to lick whiskey off your body. Your broad shoulders do things to me. Well, so does your cock. All of you. I want to lick all of you. Think we can arrange that?"

I jerked at her suggestion and dug my fingers into her. She squealed, and I covered her mouth with mine to swallow her sounds. Then I swirled my thumb around her clit, already knowing what she needed to finish the job. I changed pace, inserting three fingers and increasing the pressure. It was like we were in high school, dry humping under the bleachers, and I swore I could've gone off in my shorts with her little thrusts. "You smell so good, Fern. I can smell how turned on you are. It's sexy."

"God," she moaned into my mouth, her body clenching against me. I increased the pace, holding her tighter against me to push her over the edge. It didn't take long.

She cried against me when the orgasm hit her, her strong yet passionate body trembling on top of me. My balls were so blue I felt sick, but the expression on her beautiful face was worth it. "Shit—I could get used to seeing you fall apart on me."

"I hate to sound cliché, but this isn't normal for me." She moved off me, gently biting her lip as a frown took over her face. She looked down for a second before meeting my gaze. I liked her shyness and brazenness combination. "It's a bit surreal, Ry, the intense attraction and passion we have. I'm not used to it. It's a bit unsettling how easy it is for me to break all my rules with you."

"It's unsettling for me too, Big Cheese." I kissed her again, accepting the fact I would have a fucking boner for at least another hour. She froze and a little color left her face. "What is it?"

"Kayla. Shit! Damn you and your sexy distraction. I need to head to K233." She smoothed down her shirt, letting out a long groan that wasn't too different from her orgasm. "No more touching me or saying those lewd words."

"Lewd words?" I raised both my eyebrows, amused.

"You heard me. Now zip it. Talk about cars and shit." She slid her gaze to my dick and back up to my mouth. "Will you...be okay?"

"I'll survive," I responded, my voice not quite my normal timbre. "But I can see the outline of your nipples through your shirt and it's—"

"Shh! Stop it." She rubbed her palms over the pebbled points, giving me a stern look while doing so. If I wasn't so turned on, I would've laughed. "Talk about unsexy things. Like golf."

"Yes, ma'am. Uh...are you any good with a seven wood?"

"That was sexy, Rylan. Damn, golf is a sexy sport... I never realized. All the woods and shafts and balls..." She trailed off, zooming down the road. Regardless of my dick starting to physically hurt, I laughed. She pointed at me, scolding me, but it was cute as hell and nothing like what she intended.

"Am I allowed to accompany you to the infamous K233? You did ask me to grab a snack and while your pussy is a snack—"

"Shut your delicious mouth, Ry! I can't resist it." She swatted at me and moved from gravel to the paved road back toward the office area. It was the third time she'd used that name and while the shock had worn off, the nostalgia hadn't. "You stay put in the cart. I'll go figure it out."

"Sounds good." I smiled at her and didn't admit I wasn't fit to walk anywhere without having a real tent in my pants. Instead, I took in the surroundings. Vendors ranged from twenty-something to probably over ninety. The most random shit was everywhere. Lamps, cartoon pillows, clothes, car parts…even a five-foot-tall sculpture of a unicorn. *Why in the world would anyone want that around them?*

I was torn between following Fern's directions or asking the owner to explain why they even had that monstrosity, but laughter caught my attention. Fern had her arm slung around a gentleman not much older than me. He wore vintage Cubs gear and had a long ponytail and, while I wasn't a jealous type, I didn't like the visual of them together. He touched her and she leaned into him with an ease far beyond acquaintances. The tension in my jaw started again and I tried not to think about why.

Because that would make me insane to care. We had three more days, four more nights together. Then we'd go our separate ways. Fuck, I hadn't even asked if she was involved with anyone else…but then again, she didn't seem the type to lead men astray. Honest and hardworking, genuine and noble. Yeah—Fern would absolutely shock me if she was involved with another man and still let me do what I just did to her. I busied myself by checking email on my phone and tried not to roll my eyes at my sister's text. *Dramatic.*

Lisa: Send pictures. Mom legit thinks you're lying and not there.

Rylan: You all could've come. I offered to buy tickets.

Lisa: Hello...three monster children. And mom...well... you want her there?

Rylan: I'll send pictures. I'm in the middle of a swap-meet right now.

Lisa: Wow. I bet you're breaking out in hives being with common folk.

Rylan: Fuck off. I'll revoke my weekly babysitting.

Lisa: You do that, you die. Love you.

Nuts. Everyone in my family's nuts. I snapped a picture of the vendors setting up and sent it to Analisa and my mom just as Fern joined me in the cart. She brought her scent, her smile and her energy with her. "Thanks for waiting. I guess you couldn't really have walked around, huh? With that tenting issue?" She grinned and didn't hide the fact her gaze went straight to my crotch.

"Smart-ass. Beautiful. What can't you do?" I reached out, pulling on the end of her hair but then sat up straighter and farther away from her. She didn't seem to mind the gesture, but she didn't react to it either. "Something crossed my mind. While I'm sure I know the answer to it, I'd like to ask."

"Ask away. But we are going to get food before I keel over. Vic would tell his dad and Rich is hell to deal with when he gets all bossy." She slid into the seat, our legs touching, her tan skin right next to my khaki shorts.

"Rich?"

She turned on the golf cart and pointed to the older gentleman I'd seen her with a handful of times. He wore the same polo as the other workers and realization dawned on me. "That's Rich. He's worked for this company since dinosaurs were around. His son Vic was at K233 and used Kayla to get me to say hi. He knew I wouldn't stop by unless it was an emergency, so the two conspired against me."

She's not with that guy. "I get it. You are the Big Cheese, driving all over the place."

"Ha ha, Moneybags." She smirked in my direction and gazed at my dick. "How you doing down there?"

"Are you intentionally trying to kill me, woman?" I adjusted myself in the seat and while I wasn't as raging as before, I would still fuck her brains out the second I got the go-ahead. "You're a bit of a tease…orgasming all over me and leaving me, like this morning"

"You didn't rub one out after I left?"

"Hell no. All my orgasms are going to be with you, Fern. I'm not missing a moment with you while we're here."

"God damn it. You and your words. You're a dangerous man, Rylan. Dangerous for my body, that's for sure. Now, what was your question?"

"Right. You aren't involved with anyone, are you? Casual or not?"

"Don't have the time. Most of my love life is like this. Short-term. I like it that way so I can dedicate myself to my job." She bit the side of her lip again, frowning in thought. "I work with a lot of men and that bothers a lot of the guys I've dated. It's easier just to have hook-ups without promises, because they never last long enough to have an argument."

While her words eased the knot of tension in my neck, I didn't like thinking about her spending time naked with another guy. At all. But I sure as hell wasn't going to say that. I focused on her dedication to work, because *that* I could get behind.

"I understand that feeling. I know you didn't ask, but to be transparent, I'm not involved with anyone either."

She gave me a small smile, one of her dimples showing on her right side, and gave my arm a squeeze. "I took you for a stand-up guy and assumed you wouldn't give away these magic orgasms if you had another woman in your life. But thank you for being upfront."

"I'm in the business of truths. Lies have no place in any relationship—long-term, short-term, work-related or friends. Now, you still haven't told me why you are so into whiskey—which is just another thing about you that drives me wild—so let's get some burgers and you explain it to me. Deal?"

"You're hard to say no to, Moneybags. You're lucky I like your face."

Chapter Seven

Fern

The job pays really well and I like food. Don't punch a vendor. "Jesse — calm down."

"Don't tell me to calm down, woman. I fuckin' paid for a large lot. Twenty by thirty feet. And this ain't those measurements, so you either give me a bigger space, or give me my money and I'm leavin' this shithole."

Jesse Crew was one of those asshole men who spat when he spoke, and this was no different. Saliva flew from his mouth and a trickle of fear had my limbs trembling. It was his size that startled me. He was over six feet, well over two-hundred pounds, and while I knew we had security, he could knock me out with one punch.

"You hear me, Fern? Money. Lot. You pick," he growled and got closer to my face.

"Jesse, look. It rained last night and the painted lines blurred a bit. It's off by two inches. I'm sure it'll be — "

"Then give me two inches off the price."

"It doesn't work like that," I fired back. My radio crackled and I moved my fingers to answer it when he took a step toward me. I froze. Never in all my years working with vendors had a disgruntled patron become aggressive toward me. Sure, insults, curse words and passive-aggressive shit happened every year. But a confrontational step? *Hell. Fucking. No.* "You have five seconds to back the *fuck* away from me."

His large eyes grew two sizes and he adjusted his height to appear taller. Jesse Crew had a reputation for being a straight-up dick-shit, but, every year he paid for the spot and left when we told him. If he took a swing at me, I had no doubt every one of the surrounding vendors would step in. But that didn't solve the anxiety creeping its way down my body. I narrowed my eyes and tensed, hoping I was ready for what was going to come next.

I wasn't ready. Not at all. Not the way my entire body relaxed, or the way my chest felt heavy, like a weight rooted on my lungs.

Rylan stormed over his calm and kind demeanor gone. He positioned himself between us, putting me behind his back. He growled when he spoke. "You want to take a swing at a lady? That make you feel like a big man?"

"Who the fuck are you?" Jesse roared, the fire in his eyes dimming just a bit.

"Leave. Get in your weird ass car and leave." Rylan crossed his strong arms and spread his legs apart in a typical aggressive stance. Good god, my ovaries couldn't handle it and a small part of me whimpered.

Jesse didn't take well to Rylan's demands and curled his lip in my direction. I shook my head and pointed with my thumb to Rylan. "You come at me, you'll be arrested on the spot. You feel like dancing with this guy, it's your ass getting beat. Make the smart decision here, Jesse."

He squeezed his fists at his sides, a vein bulging in his neck to the point I thought it might burst. Then, he screamed like a goddamn banshee, stomped to his obnoxious large red truck and yelled for everyone to hear, "Fuck this place. I don't need this shit."

Damp mud from the storm flew all over the area when he sped off, but the tension that had wedged itself in my muscles left with him. He caused issues year after year, and with this? He'd be banned. Rylan faced me with a guilty expression, his hands already going to my shoulders. "I'm sorry for stepping on your toes. I know you can handle anything, but I couldn't stay quiet. He was a fucking dick."

I couldn't stop my smile. No one had stood up for me before, at least like that. And Rylan wouldn't be on the list of guys who didn't embrace strong women. If anything, he made my alpha-woman personality seem sexy. This time, I reached out and gave his wrist a squeeze. "Thank you. Really. It was a pleasant surprise. Apparently, I liked you standing up for me. I did not expect that."

The guilty expression shifted into warmth, like he was proud of me. I didn't like the way my body reacted to his grin and I stretched my arms over my head. The crowd grew around us and soon a bunch of old-timers marched up and patted Rylan on the back. Jason Levitt, a sixty-year-old vintage poster collector I had known for six years, gave me a pointed look. "I'm glad you did that, young man. He's a piece of shit but he's in the business with us. He has some pull at the other shows, you know, the smaller ones, so we couldn't afford to cut ties. Sorry we didn't do something, Fernie."

Paul, another longtime vender, put his hand on my back with a forlorn look. "You all right, Fernie? You need a Bud?"

I laughed. "You know I don't like drinking that shit."

"Come on, bring your man friend and have a drink. You can take a ten-minute break."

And that was how I found myself sitting in the back of a '95 Chevy pick-up truck, surrounded by '50s diner pieces and drinking piss beer with seven men. Six were older than sixty, missing teeth and smelled like tobacco, but the seventh one was the cherry on top. Rylan sat next to me, our thighs touching, and he looked right at home and nothing like Mr. Moneybags, dressed in a black shirt and casual shorts. He threw his head back and laughed at some sexual comment Paul made, leaning his shoulder into mine as he grinned. "This is awesome."

"The beer, the company or the drama?" I held up the red can and clinked it against his. His gaze dropped to my mouth for a second before we both took a long sip. The disgusting taste didn't bother me as much as it normally did — the company was worth it.

"This is nothing like I expected."

"What's that now, slick?" Jason barked at the newest member of our crew. Rylan shifted his attention to the older gentleman and the smile never left his face.

"I'm a first timer here. It's fucking fantastic."

"Of course it is. It's a bunch of knuckleheads who drink beer, talk shit and hopefully leave with a little money. There's not much more to life than that." He chugged the rest of his beer and crushed it in his hand. "Ain't that right, Fernie?"

"Damn straight, Jason." I finished the rest of my beer and pointed from Jason to Rylan. "Tell you what. Jason, Paul, can y'all show Rylan around? Give him the scoop on everybody?"

"Someone's gotta. There's rules here. The way of the land."

Rylan narrowed his eyes at me, but I just threw him a wink. I patted his shoulder and waved to the rest of the guys. "Some of us have to work...but I'll see you guys later."

"Ms. Laughlin?" Rylan asked after I took a couple of steps away from their crew. He ran his hand through his messy hair and a small part of me, unfamiliar and foreign, wanted to take a picture of him like that. His handsome face a little sunburned, his clothes covered in dust and drinking a good old-fashioned American beer.

"Yes?"

"You owe me that whiskey."

"That I do." I ran my teeth over my bottom lip, excitement bursting in my belly. "Trust me, I'll find you later."

* * * *

The warm feeling in my chest didn't last long—Christine and Andrew were bitching about sales and refusing to look me in the eye when I walked into the offices. Christine might have been a bit flaky, but I had never heard her use such an aggressive tone with our boss and while it startled me, I gave up trying to figure out what was going on with them. The show hadn't even started...and I had a hot guy waiting for me.

My typical drive to the hotel included going over every detail, every hiccup that could happen, and creating an action plan to fix it. But for the first time, I thought about Rylan and all the ways he could distract me, pleasure me and, damn, excitement coursed through me.

My room was three floors above his and I quickly showered and changed into a loose dress — braless for practical reasons — and grabbed the amber bottle. The elevator ride took a minute and soon enough, I took the keycard and opened the door. The lack of nerves or second-guessing was incredible — instead there was confidence and anticipation of seeing a guy I enjoyed spending time with. It was liberating as hell, knowing he trusted me enough to use his body. "Moneybags, you in here?"

I was met with his cologne, a delicious and intoxicating scent, and took ten steps into the room. He leaned against the bedframe, headphones in as he studied something on his laptop. Goddamn, he was a pretty picture with his dark eyebrows and tan skin. I hit the bottle against the dresser, and he glanced up. The shift in his expression might've been my favorite three seconds ever. His face lit up — his warm eyes widening, his smile stretching across his entire face and he set the laptop on the side table, removing all evidence of him working.

He didn't disappoint. His hands went to my hips, his lips to my mouth and every single worry about the show left me. It was just him. "Mm. I hate to be clingy, but it's twenty minutes after nine. I was getting desperate."

"Yeah?" I set the bottle down and wrapped my arms around his neck. I liked this position, where I could pull him to me. "I took the world's fastest shower."

"You really shouldn't have even worn this dress." He gave me a wicked grin before lifting the hem of it and pulling it over my head. "Goddamn. You'd think I've never seen your tits before, but every time..."

I shivered at his words, the tone of his voice and his attention. It was like he saw nothing else besides me, and *fuck* I liked it. But I had plans. "Nah, you go lie on the bed."

"Yes, Ms. Laughlin." He bit down on my nipple for a quick second, sucking it in his warm mouth in a torturous way, before he jumped onto the bed. He didn't wait a second before slipping off his loose shorts, blessing me with his toned, naked body. "Are you going to dance for me?"

"Ah, no. I draw the line there. But...I am going to lick whiskey off your body. You know, like we discussed." I gave him a coy smile and shimmied a little.

He flared his nostrils with a quick intake of breath and I felt drunk on power. The bottle of whiskey hung from my hand and I slid the top off with ease. "Does that sound like a plan, Ry?"

He gulped, his massive chest heaving with his ragged breath. Something about him reminded me of the whiskey—the sweet sherry notes remained on my palate for days after taking a sip, and he would too. His voice was low and gravelly when he said, "You're dangerous."

I gave him the cockiest smile I could muster and let a little of the whiskey drip on his stomach. It flowed down his hard muscles, onto the bed a little bit, and down to his massive cock. He hissed and I set the bottle on the table next to the bed. "My body is shaking with need right now, Rylan. Your body and whiskey might be by favorite combination ever."

"Uh, fuck. Yeah. Me too," he grunted. His strangled voice gave me even more confidence and pleasure, knowing this affected us both.

I crawled onto him but decided to try something last-minute. Instead of remaining at the end of the bed, I made sure my ass faced his face. I arched my back when I brought my tongue to his abs and I hoped he'd take the hint. Oh, he sure did.

He buried his mouth into my throbbing pussy, sucking and biting down on my swollen labia just as I took his whiskey-flavored cock into my mouth. It was a lethal combination, his taste and the burn of the leathery whiskey. I took him entirely, his excessive size hitting the back of my throat. He groaned, humming into my core, and I was sure my eyes were going to roll back into my head.

Nope. Now they were going to, when he spread my ass cheeks apart, dragging his tongue farther up and licking every single part of me. It was sensual, beyond anything I had experienced, and I shook with an explosive orgasm. But he didn't let me stop. He continued the thrusting of his tongue, reaching out with his hands and pinching the end of my taut nipples. It was an explosion of sensations.

The whiskey.

Rylan's tongue.

Rylan's fingers.

His cock in my mouth.

I fell apart completely. The loss of control should've terrified me, but instead I felt empowered. He took care of me in every way, sexually, and I'd never had a lover so dedicated to the woman's pleasure. "Fucking Christ, Rylan."

"Here, lie back on the bed, feisty." His strangled voice was kind, yet still held a control I didn't want to disobey. I shivered, remembering the scene from earlier in the day where he'd stood up for me. "I promise it'll be worth it."

"I trust you," I moaned. The high from the orgasm still shook me and I didn't fight him when he repositioned me to lie on my back. I opened my eyes and found him grinning wickedly at me. "What?"

"You look real good after an orgasm. You get these wild eyes and a slight blush on your cheeks. You're a hard woman to walk away from, I'll tell you that." He picked up the bottle of whiskey and took a swig, letting the cold liquid drip from his mouth onto my neck. Goosebumps broke out down my spine when he nipped at the sensitive skin, licking the alcohol up. "Now, what's your favorite thing about whiskey?"

"Before right now, I'd say the aftertaste. Now, it's all about the experience," I replied into his hair. He leaned over, sheathed himself in protection and grabbed another sip. I admired his back muscles and wondered how he had them when he worked on computers, but hell, I wasn't complaining.

"I'm going to have to agree with you there. Now, I'm going to be honest with you," he spoke softly and covered my body with his. He ran his tongue down the center of my chest, pressing a kiss right above my heart. The gesture was like a punch to the gut, but he didn't give me time to react. "I'm not going to last more than a couple minutes with how fucking sexy you are. But the second time, I'll make it more worthwhile."

I giggled, digging my fingers into his back when he slowly slipped inside me. "God, it's about time."

"Shut up, Fern. I'm barely holding on. You're tight as hell." He thrust, clenching his entire body and giving me the perfect handful of ass to grab. I arched my hips up, giving him the perfect angle to my G-spot, and he had no issue finding it. We found a rhythm, the perfect combination of give and take. Sweat pooled between our bodies, our haggard breaths the only sound in the room. The tobacco and woodsy smell from the whiskey combined with the sweat from our skin, the scent clouding my nose, and fuck, it was the best combination ever.

"Grip my ass, Rylan," I demanded as a slow burn formed in my gut. He reached around and dug his fingers into the curve of my ass, kneaded the skin and gripped me harder. It gave the right pressure, and the beginning of my orgasm formed. "*Yes*. I'm close."

"Working, naked — doesn't matter what you do, you have me enraptured, feisty."

He said the words between thrusts and I came around him, my eyes stinging at the power of the orgasm. I cried out, barely able to hold on to him as wave after wave of pleasure hit me. I said his name, then he kissed the hell out of me. It had never been like this before, but I didn't have time to tell him that. He was close — his back tensed and he buried his face into my neck. I wrapped my legs around his waist, pulling him closer, and it did the trick. He moaned my name, the sound animalistic, and spilled into me. "Jesus."

"You have me drugged on you." My voice came out all husky and deep. It matched my mood and I couldn't wait for more. With him, nothing else mattered.

He let out a slow laugh, slipping out of me with a gentleness that could've broken the strongest woman. He pressed a kiss on the skin just above my belly button—a gesture so sweet I had the urge to run. But then he whistled and brought his gaze to my pussy. "Best. Fucking. Ever."

"That, Mr. Moneybags, we can agree on."

He threw away the condom and raised his eyebrows at me, pointing to the bottle. "Now, I say we enjoy a nice drink when we recover from round one."

"How many rounds should I expect from you, Mr. Cirula?" I brought the sheet up to cover my breasts and reached for the bottle. But he snatched the sheet off me and shook his head.

"Naked whiskey drinks. That's my rule. When you're in my room, we're naked."

"I see why your company is successful—you create awesome rules." I smiled at him, comfortably crossing my legs and pouring a glass for him.

"That I do." He took the glass and joined me against the headboard. "Now, tell me why you came in here with stress all over your body."

"You...you can tell?" *Well fuck.*

"Yeah. I've been staring at you every second I can the past forty-eight hours. I see something's wrong. Now, spill it, Big Cheese. Maybe I can help."

Chapter Eight

Rylan

Three things I learned about Fern in three fingers of Glendronach 18 — her favorite uncle got her hooked on expensive whiskey, she got defensive about her job and she was cute as fuck when she got flustered. It took a lot of effort to not laugh when she paced the room, butt-ass naked with her perky, bouncy tits, rambling about her bullshit bosses. She stopped in front of the TV, put her hands on her hips and glared at me.

I pressed my lips together until the urge to chuckle went away. She didn't notice my struggle, thankfully. "Have you confronted them about this?"

"I've tried, Rylan. Every time I approach them to talk about sales, or vendor profits or anything, *fuck*, they busy off. And it's weird. They have all these meetings with Christine's daughter...that's peculiar, right? We used to all meet, the three of us, as president and two VPs, but now, I'm left out of the discussions. Sure, the owners and their Silvas bring in most of the money but...I'd like to think we make a shit-ton of money from the other side of the show." She took a long breath, poured another finger of the Glendronach and shot it back. Her blue eyes shifted to a dark navy—like the sky right as the sun sets—and she pursed her lips at me. "What do you think?"

"If you're a board of three, no decisions regarding the company can be made. That's a normal policy to follow—do you have a constitution? A business plan? Anything like that or is it just you three on the governing board?" I frowned into my glass, an uneasy feeling forming in my gut. Most people didn't know how difficult it was to manage a business, but as soon as anything shady happened, it was damn hard to regain ground. *Poor Fern.*

"No. None of those. And I *know* that's a normal policy to follow." She pushed her hair up into a messy ponytail again, loose pieces framing her face. Despite her fast-changing expression, she was beautiful. "I'm not an idiot."

"Woah, I have no doubt you're not an idiot. I'm playing devil's advocate here. I know if two of us at my company tried to make a decision without the rest of the board, our asses would be fried, maybe even fired." I took a sip, enjoying the woodsy taste, but froze when her gaze narrowed at me. "You somehow even look hotter when you're mad."

"Don't charm me, Rylan." She pressed two fingers into her forehead and bit down on her lip, worry and unease clear in her eyes. "Do you think they are planning to fire me, regardless of the revenue? Andrew keeps mentioning the sales aren't what they need to be and brushes me off when I explain how much more I've helped bring in this year."

"Hmm," I took my time replying, trying to think of the best way to advise her. It didn't sound good. A ball of dread formed in my stomach. In the short time I'd known her, I'd seen she clearly loved her job. And she was good at it. Hell, if I felt like I was being pushed out...I'd lose my goddamn mind. "When did this start? Them meeting without you?"

"I was so busy getting ready for the show... I'm not sure. Maybe this month?" She poured another finger and took a sip, humming in pleasure. Her sounds were the fucking best, but I focused on her and her problem. They took precedence over my dick. "No, really just this week. And why is Marla there?"

"What does she do? Could she be talking about her job? No offense to her, but I haven't seen her working anywhere." Not that I was looking, because I wasn't. I did like observing and had an almost photographic memory and I hadn't seen her since that first day.

Fern rolled her eyes and her lips quirked up a bit. "Yeah...she's the office flirt and sometimes takes pictures. Generally, it gets put on me. I don't mind though. It's fun and I know everyone—"

"And everyone respects you. I imagine you get better pictures than she would."

Her expression warmed and I was glad I'd said it. Her pride was clear and well-earned. "Thank you for saying that. I needed to hear it. I hate feeling inferior, but...something about them is bothering me. Especially when Andrew said I was going to be fired if I didn't raise revenue by at least five percent, which is a hard—"

"Excuse me?"

"What?" She paled and widened her eyes. "Why do you—what's wrong?"

I shook my head, hoping I'd heard her wrong. "He expects you, and you alone, to raise over five percent of total profit, or you're fired? What the fuck?"

She blinked a couple of times, her posture straightening. I recognized it, her battle stance. But her anger was misplaced. "I am damn good at my job and I can surely help raise revenue, Rylan. I might not be a millionaire, but fuck. I can market and help—"

"Fern." My temper flared a bit at her jab at my wealth. My voice must've startled her because she stopped talking and a flash of guilt crossed her face. "How much did Cruising Silvas make last year? Two million?"

She blanched but nodded. "Yeah, roughly."

"Your boss expects you to increase profit by one hundred thousand...from the vendor side of the show? How much do they pay for a lot, one hundred? Four lots, one hundred each...that's four thousand. Fern. The reality of that is not possible."

Her expression shifted again, whatever intimacy we had that day that extended beyond the bedroom disappearing. It was as if I could hear the walls she was building, shoving me out one second at a time. "Thanks for the math lesson."

"Look, I'm sorry." I set my glass on the side table and walked up to her, rubbing my hands down her arms. "I overstepped a boundary. You are incredible at what you do, and if it was up to me, you'd run the show. Honestly, I'm not sure how you don't own your own company. If you want to talk business, I'll listen. But until you ask for my advice, I'll keep quiet."

She remained stiff as her intelligent gaze scanned my face for something. She didn't find it and I bent low enough to kiss the spot under her jaw. She always trembled when I brought my lips to it, and this time was no different. "We're good together and I want to continue to embrace our wild hotel-and-Silvas sex for the week. Forgive me?"

She closed her eyes for a couple of seconds, then deflated. Her posture relaxed and a spark came back into her eyes. "You're right. I should be the one sorry. You are most certainly not the enemy. It's just too personal to talk about. I'd rather enjoy your body in the short time I have with you, you know?"

"I will never say no to that. Honestly, I had to use the sheet to cover my cock when you were getting all pissed. It turned me on."

"You have the sex drive of a horny teenager," she said with a slight giggle. Her expression went back to normal, the one that radiated confidence and joy. She brought her hand to my dick and gave it a slight stroke. "Seriously?"

"It's all you, Big Cheese. I can't decide if it's your fantastic tits, your mouth or your taste in whiskey. Whatever it is, I'm hooked." I trailed my fingers down her neck, over her collarbone and down the center of her tits. We both watched while I traced the outline of her dusky pink nipples, already pointed and desperate to be sucked. "Your body is addictive."

"Your damn words again, getting me all hot. New rule — no more talking about work. Just sex." She began licking my neck, going lower and lower until she got right above my cock. "Can you get behind that rule?"

"Fuck yeah. Let's start now."

* * * *

My entire body needed sleep. My face hurt, my eyes barely able to stay open. But my dick felt great. The lack of sleep would knock me on my ass at the end of the week, and Fern was worth every fucking second, but I needed to hook an IV of caffeine into me to get through the day. The noodlers were a bunch of young twenty-something guys who had multiple Red Bulls in their pockets. A small part of me wanted to buy one off them, but that shit was not good for the body. "Mr. Cirula, you're up next."

"Thanks, kid," I said with a gruff voice. I sounded eighty, not like a fit thirty-five-year-old. I cleared my throat and started Rayme's engine. It roared, the entire vehicle shaking and rattling my teeth in my jaw. There wasn't any air conditioning in the vintage car and the humid air was already stifling. But...I felt him. My dad. The stories the car had. If I closed my eyes and focused, I swore I could smell his old cologne he'd worn for fifty years. Fuck—I did not want to get feelings and shit when I had teenagers waving pool noodles at me. I blamed the lack of sleep and the lack of coffee, because drinks were not allowed in the car.

A punk with a straw hat waved me on, holding two pool noodles. They were bright green and he crooked his finger at me until I drove the bumper into the foam. "There you go, sir. You're in position for judging."

"Huh. The noodles do work, then." I got out of the car and nodded at its position. It fit perfectly in the two lines allotted for the judging. *Interesting.* "I thought she was full of shit."

The kid laughed and gave me a patronizing look. "They work, sir. This might be your first time here, but we've been doing the noodles for years. Good luck with the judging." He gave a wave and took his noodles and energy to the next guy in line. That left me with three hours until the show started and while I was tempted to drive back to the hotel to sleep, I really could get some work done. I had investors trying to reschedule a conference call to talk about bids and while my brain wasn't in full gear, setting up the conference would be mindless enough. Christine had given me permission to use the little offices right next to the judging field and I walked in and found an empty cubicle.

I put on my headphones and dove in, the thrill of having companies use my product never getting old, even after a decade of pouring my soul into the business. Technology and creating were my thing, not cars, and it was a nice break from the show.

I was through about forty emails when the door opened and hushed voices carried over the short plaster wall. I didn't recognize the first one, but I didn't have a problem figuring out who it was — Andrew and Christine, Fern's bosses. I turned off my music and muted my computer. They shouted at each other and I wasn't sure how long they had already been out there. I did know it was too late for me to walk out, but I kept the headphones in. If I had to use them as a shield, I would.

"If her husband found out, Andrew…this is bad. How could you do this?" Christine whined, the sound clashing with my interpretation of her. Her voice was lethal, frightening and nothing of the soft, needy woman I talked to the previous day. My nerves were on edge.

"I didn't mean for it to happen, Christine. *Fuck!* How did you even know?" Andrew's voice had a menacing tone to it, his anger and threats sneaking through. Someone slammed something metal onto a table. A can, maybe?

"I know my daughter has affairs, but with my fucking boss? The boss who was about to fire me? Are you kidding? Do you even have a soul anymore or was it overtaken by your dick?"

"Watch how you talk to me, Christine. I'm still in charge of your career."

I froze. *Poor Fern.* Her suspicions were correct, but she just had no idea how fucked up it was. Fury bubbled in my blood, but I couldn't do a thing. I kept listening, praying something made sense about this. *Andrew and Marla? What the fuck?*

Who sleeps with their VP's daughter?

"You can't fire me," Christine replied and let out maniacal laugh. "If you fire me, I'll sue you and sic her husband on you. He's wealthy and ripped — he doesn't like when Marla has her flings and I just can't believe she roped you into one. And Jesus, Andrew, you made us all sign agreements not to have relationships with anyone on staff, and you sleep with my goddamn daughter? Here? When I was feet away? You're a monster."

"Lower your voice," he demanded in the same threatening tone. "No one will find out. We're having fun. We get each other, okay? Marla and I...it's different. Don't worry about us, got it?" He stopped speaking and shuffled something. Someone — my guess was Christine — gasped and hit something hard.

"What is this? Y-you're going to *fire* poor Fern to protect Marla?"

"Lower your voice, Christine."

"Are you kidding? Do you ever care about this company at all?" Her voice broke, but I felt no sympathy for her. If Christine knew about this and didn't tell Fern... *My god.*

"This company is *mine* and if you want to keep your insurance, your salary, hell, the car I loaned you, you'll keep your mouth shut. I know you fudge your hour sheets each week to make ends meet. I also know you're below average at actually making us any money. I never cared before, but I can retract those checks. Watch me, Christine. As far as Fern, she'll land on her feet. But trust me, if you say a word to her, it'll be both your asses out of work and I know you need the money."

She didn't respond to his last threat, huffing and storming out of the makeshift offices. I didn't move a muscle until Andrew's footsteps echoed through the foyer, the door opening and him walking out into the show. I rubbed the back of my neck, completely out of my element. Fern didn't want to talk about business, but she was going to get fired because her boss was a dick and sleeping with Christine's married daughter.

Christine was forced to keep her mouth shut if she wanted a job, and she sounded desperate. This was a goddamn telenovela and my computational brain spun, trying to find a practical solution that made sense.

What the fuck am I supposed to do?

Chapter Nine

Fern

Showtime, baby. I propped my feet up on the dashboard of my golf cart and sipped my scalding hot and delicious coffee. My mood had almost nothing to do with Rylan and waking up with his head between my legs...or the shower we spent thirty minutes in...or the fact that he'd *felt* like bringing me a cup of coffee at the entrance tent. *Nope.* I blamed the beautiful weather, the heavy stream of people entering the event and the zero issues that had come up.

"Big Cheese, tell me that smile on your face has something to do with the handsome hunk following you around." Kayla plopped down next to me on the seat. I bit down to prevent a smile, but she hit her shoulder against mine. "Hey, I'm jealous as hell. You deserve to look this happy all the time. He must be giving it real good."

"*Kayla!*" I scolded her and made sure no one was around us. The part-time helpers we'd hired stood at the major intersection, handing out pamphlets with directions and helped direct the Silvas where to park. Because, yes, if someone drove a Silvas to the show, they got VIP parking. But if someone drove a Silvas that was the year we were celebrating, like the '68, then they got even better parking right in the center. "Watch it, kid."

She raised her eyebrows and gave me a fake-ass shrug. "So, how is he?"

I tensed, thought of all the reasons this was inappropriate. She was my employee and we had a strict no-relationship policy, but I'd known Kayla since she was sixteen and she'd been my right-hand woman for the past eight years. "Let's just say, it's been a hell of a good week."

"Atta girl. Get it, boss."

I shoved her out of the cart with a laugh. "Go work. I pay you to do things."

"At least one of us gets to *do* fun things."

"I'll fire your ass, Kay."

She flipped me off with a big smirk and joined the two guys at the intersection—there were boxes of freebies every person got when they arrived and they were a bitch to hand out. Membership pins, anniversary pennants, cards—like baseball cards—with models and makes that were big that year, and towels. I was damn glad I didn't have to stand there and do that, but my moment of joy was gone. The radio crackled and Gary's worried voice carried over.

"Fern, we need you out on the goldfields."

"On it, be right there." I clipped the radio on my collar and took off toward the area where all the Silvas could park. It was in the center of the event, so owners, vendors, patrons and judges could see the mass of Silvas there. It took a good ten minutes to arrive with all the foot traffic, which was great for sales, but not for driving a golf cart. Gary stood there, his hands on his hips and a forlorn expression on his weathered face. My stomach sank, my entire back tensing with worry about what could've happened. *Has someone hit a Silvas? Was there a fight?* "What is it?"

"Remember that rain?" He scrunched his nose and jutted his chin toward the grass.

I scanned the field for a puddle but didn't see anything related to rain. "Sure, what about it?"

"The semi with the 'Vas for sale got stuck in the wet grass when he was unloading and, well… Come on. Follow me." He took off and I followed, my long legs able to keep up with his stride. He pointed as we passed four rows of perfectly parked '67s but then I gasped. *Fucking shit.* The semi had dug itself into the ground, with the grass torn up and mud sprayed everywhere. It covered at least ten cars, two vendor tents and the poor grass was destroyed. Completely destroyed and my first thought annoyed me — the price of the grass.

"What are we going to do, Fern? Vendors are pissed, the ground crew is going to chew me out, and shit…how do we get the semi out? He's blocking traffic and causing a scene."

It took ten seconds for my thoughts to stop spinning and I formed a plan. *One step at a time.* I found my radio and called for Karl. "Karl, my guy, can you round up about ten of the noodlers or any helpers, even the Boy Scouts volunteering? Bring water, rags and buckets and meet us on the goldfield."

"You got it, Fernie."

I stared at Gary now. "Instruct the helpers to wipe down all the mud from the vendors and the tents. As far as the cars...have the kids stand by the car and volunteer to clean them when the owners return. That part's hard without having their permission to clean."

"No, that works. Yeah." He frowned and rubbed the back of his neck a bit before nodding. "That could solve one issue. What about the semi?"

"Tow truck. Call Chas — he's the grounds guy, yeah?"

"Yup. Think a tow can help?"

"It'll at least give it leverage. Shit, do we have any plywood or anything we could wedge behind the wheel?" I'd seen it on a YouTube video once and while it was wild, it could work. "I can make a run to buy some. At this rate, I might have to go buy some sod."

"What? You're going to buy grass? What in the world?"

"This area is the middle of the show. We cannot have a bald patch here. The temporary grass will serve its purpose for the week." A moment of panic hit me — we were doing an aerial shot of the event the next day to help get promote the show online. We'd even talked about doing a live stream from a droid. *Shit.* "Kayla, you there?"

"You got it, Big Cheese. What's up?"

"You're in charge for an hour. Can you handle it?" I shared a glance with Gary. Kayla, Gary and I ran the entire show outside the judging-and-owners part and we rocked it, but everyone got nervous when I wasn't there. But she responded like the badass I knew her to be.

"You got it. Do what you gotta do, boo boo."

I rolled my eyes but her humor was well timed and gave me a bit of relief. She could handle anything, really. "I'll run out for a what, two by four or so and how much grass?"

"Two pallets, about four hundred dollars or so. That should work." Gary scanned the grounds and nodded his head toward the semi driver. "I'm going to tell Mac the plan and fend off the unhappy vendors. Possibly get the tow truck if I can."

He took off just when the volunteers showed up with towels and I could breathe a little easier — one crisis averted. I thanked them all, instructed them on what to do, and sped off toward the garages where employees parked. The nearest Home Depot was twenty minutes south and I let out a small cuss word when I realized my keys were in the office — a good three-minute jog away.

I didn't get ten steps in when someone called out to me. "Fern — hey, what's wrong?"

I spun toward the voice, a brief sense of relief and happiness going through me when Rylan's concerned face met mine. My racing heart was because I was running, and not at all because of *him*. "We have a grass issue. I'm going to buy some."

"I'm sorry, you're going to buy grass?" His eyebrows bunched together, forming a slight line between them. It was cute. Then he lowered his voice and stepped closer to me "Like, marijuana?"

I cackled, reaching out and using his shoulder to support my weight. "Oh my god. I needed that. No. Adorable answer, you naïve, silly man. Literally, a grass issue. The lawn is torn up and a semi is stuck. I need to buy a pallet of sod and some wood."

"I can help with some wood," he replied, his voice getting all low and husky. I didn't have time to react and he wiped the smirk from his face. "Sorry, not the time. Want help? I know I don't look like it, but I've helped out with quite a bit of remodeling and know my way around a Lowe's. After all, they really are just man malls."

"Sure, yeah. Come on. My keys are in the office — shit! I can't fit a pallet in my car!" Panic bubbled up, making my thoughts blur together, but he put a warm hand against my back, soothing me.

"Let's take my SUV. I can unhitch the trailer and use the extra space. Come on, Big Cheese. Help me help you." He grinned again and I swore I felt it in my toes. A small part of me, almost non-existent, felt bad about lashing out at him about my job. But this wasn't the place to talk about it. We had a grass issue.

* * * *

I relaxed into his passenger seat an hour later, his cologne offering a brief escape from the humid smells of grass in the back. I spared him a quick glance at the wheel, admiring his sharp jawline and the way-past-five-o-clock shadow that increased each day. Some unknown feeling went through me, a little stronger than desire and close to curiosity. *What about him has me so interested and tied up in knots? His good looks? His charm?*

"Feisty, I can feel you staring at me. Feel free to touch."

"Thanks for the invitation," I replied with a chuckle. I wasn't embarrassed at all at getting caught. That was the thing about him — I felt more alive, more *me* when I was with him than with any other man. "If I wasn't so goddamn worried about the grass, then I would. I'd even try to convince you for some car nookie."

"Car nookie?" He widened his eyes and shook with laughter. "I shouldn't get excited when you use those words, but hell. I am."

"Watching you command everyone in the store, not letting them try to stall us with their salesperson bullshit. It was hot, man. Tell me, what sort of remodeling have you done?"

"My sister has three monster children. I love them, but they're crazy and her small house was not suitable to raise them. I helped her husband with an addition, giving them three more rooms. Plus, uh, my dad passed away recently and the house needed severe updates before we could put it on the market." His voice was a little off when speaking about his dad, less joyful than the one I had gotten used to. I fought the urge to comfort him. He didn't sense my unease, and kept talking. I held on to his every word, wanting to know everything about him.

"It was rough, losing him. Sudden. He was fine, traveling to these goddamn car shows all over the US. I wasn't ready for him to go. We had unsolved issues." He released a long breath and gave me a quick glance. "Sorry, this isn't great talk when you have a lot of work stuff going on."

"No, go ahead. I'm curious." *Fuck it.* I reached out and put my hand on his knee. "Your dad was into Silvas? Is that how you got involved? Not that I'm complaining."

He released a quick breath, bordering on a laugh, and squeezed my hand in response. He kept his there, covering mine, and I got an attack of butterflies in my stomach. I hadn't held hands with anyone since…three years ago. Even then, it had felt weird, almost forced, to show displays of affection. But with Rylan…I wanted it. It was comforting, to both of us, and each time his thumb brushed against my wrist, a jolt of awareness traveled up my arm.

He spoke again, pulling my attention from my minor freak-out mode. "The '67 I have was his. Rayme. God, he named his cars and talked about finally entering it into Accreditation when he was sixty...but he never made it. I did it for him. My mom and sister pushed me to do it, but I held off as long as I could. We didn't... Cars aren't my thing but I caved in the end. To fulfill his wishes, you know?"

"There are worse reasons to enter. I'll have you know, the owners all have names for their Silvas. Crazier names than Rayme. There've been Daisys, Foxys, Guacamole... I swear." That earned me a small chuckle—my goal. "I think it's noble, Rylan. You're honoring your father by entering. I mean, I knew you weren't a car guy. For one, you aren't obsessed with it and wearing polos with the 'Va logo on it and two, you haven't spent every free second either cleaning the car, talking to the car or stalking the judges to get on their good side."

"Do people wear polos with the logo?"

"There's an entire store on the south part of the event with all Silvas branded clothing. You can also find the latest and greatest Cruising Silvas gear. I saw you eyeing my shirt—probably my boobs—but still, you can purchase this for the low price of forty dollars. And it comes in any color you fancy. White, black, purple, teal. Name it, baby, and it's yours."

"Totally checking out your tits. Do you—well, I have a favor to ask of you." He pulled into the event, slowing down the SUV and coming to a stop before heading down the alley to park. "It seems stupid—"

"What is it?" I asked in the kindest voice I had. He looked so tortured, his eyes hooded and his jaw tensing every couple of seconds.

"I want the experience. Like my dad. I'm not a fan of cars. Hell, I either work from home or take the EL in Chicago to go places. But he loved them and I want to try."

Goddamn. My heart clenched. My throat tightened, and I needed a large glass of water. I coughed, giving myself another second to get my emotions in check, and nodded. "I need to finish this issue on the field, but I'll find you after. I can show you a good time."

"Can't wait." He leaned over, cupped my chin and forced me to look at him. Sadness, warmth and maybe guilt swirled in his eyes and I had to blink a couple of times to break the seriousness of his gaze. He didn't speak, the air stifling around us as he closed the distance between our mouths. It was a sweet kiss, not a claim or a promise of more later. It was gentle, his lips pressing against mine in no hurry. He kissed me three more times before moving the car to the garage, the silence building the entire time.

The kiss wasn't part of our deal. The sweetness most definitely wasn't. Nor were the conversations about our past. Yet...I liked all of it and craved more of the tenderness, the soft kisses with little secrets coming out. He parked and, in a voice full of emotion, I mumbled, "Thanks for the help."

"I like helping you. Now, find me later for the good time you promised," he responded and gave me a wink. By god, I wanted to strip him down then and there to give him a good time — the first time work hadn't come first for me.

Shit. I needed to pull myself together. Guys like Rylan were delicious distractions and, with all the weird shit with my bosses, I needed to stay focused.

Chapter Ten

Rylan

My sister always said it took a big man to admit when a woman was stronger than him, and it had never made sense until now. Fern was stronger — her command of people, her ability to compartmentalize tasks and the innate confidence with which she held herself. I couldn't stop watching her. Bent low, laying sod on the mud with dirt all over her legs, she was the most beautiful woman I had ever seen. And I'd seen quite a few of them, with all the blind dates, the set-ups and the money-seeking women more attracted to my wealth than me. That was the difference with her. She didn't really care about my job. It pleased me more than she realized. That had to be why I was so drawn to her sounds and smiles. She was satisfied with her own career — mine didn't matter to her. Content with my realization as to why I was so goddamn into her, I relaxed.

A group of guys dressed in matching polos approached her. She pointed to the grass, said something that had them all laughing and they nodded at her. *Huh.* It was her management of people, her kindness to them. She'd make a hell of an owner, and the idea made perfect sense. Fern should run the *entire* show, not just the operation side.

The thought took hold and I left her to figure out the grass issue to go check on Rayme. She remained where I'd parked her, and I snapped a couple of pictures to send to my sister and Mom. They responded with thumbs-up and the urge to complain and roll my eyes went away.

I wanted to understand it more, what Christine did for the company, and maybe mess with her a bit. She should be the one to tell Fern the truth, not me. Christine — the one being blackmailed by Andrew — laughed with one of the judges and a wave of disgust had me cringing.

Every time Fern smiled, I felt the lie buried in my chest. Dishonest people had no place in my life and keeping something from her felt awful. A light pounding began in the base of my skull and I rubbed it, hoping it would relieve the tension, but nothing happened. *Another guilt-ache. Fuck.* I marched up to Christine and waited for her to see me. Her entire face lit up and she turned her whole body toward me, her appreciative gaze creeping me out. I cringed. "Hi, Mr. Cirula. What can I do for you?"

I plastered on a smile, hoping it looked normal and not like a psychopath's. "I'm curious. I haven't been to one of these shows before and the entire judging and Accreditation process puzzles me. How do you run registration and set it up?"

Her eyes lit up and she didn't hide the excitement in her voice. "Oh, we have applications online where you register your car and provide all the information to prove it's yours. You'd be surprised how many VINs are fake and the owners don't even know it!"

I stared at her without smiling and she continued. "Once you provide all the information, we get everything set up for the judges. They have to go through quite extensive training to be certified for this event and the judges are divided into teams—each team has a head judge and they do the final tallying."

"Okay, interesting." My curiosity wasn't satisfied and I adjusted my position, crossing my arms. "Is there a limit for the number of cars an owner can enter?"

"Oh, no. You can enter as many as you'd like." She beamed and leaned closer. "Did you have other cars and not enter them? I think we can squeeze you in if you'd like, Mr. Cirula."

"Ah, no. I'm good. Just the one." I hoped to end the conversation there, but she persisted.

"Did you have any more questions or are you satisfied?"

I frowned. She didn't need to make that question sound so crude. But I wanted to understand more aspects of the show to try and convince Fern to take over the entire thing...but once again, my brain and actions weren't on the same page. I backtracked. "I'm a money guy. Where do most of the profits come from?"

"Depends on the year, but mainly the Accreditation. The vendors and sponsors offer a nice benefit, too."

"Does Ms. Laughlin handle the sponsors?"

"Sure does. She got Chevy to be here this year and they paid a pretty price." Her gaze went to the ground and she shifted her weight—a telltale sign she wanted to avoid this topic of conversation. While I prided myself on being a savvy businessman, I got my shots in when I could. I lowered my voice, almost whispering to her. Her lips parted, but I paid no attention.

"It'd sure be a shame if Fern wasn't able to return next year, huh?"

Then I left her. I didn't have to imagine her paled face or wide eyes. Her reflection was in the window of the offices and it brought me a little bit of joy to see her flustered. But hell, Fern did everything for the show and was going to be let go because a guy couldn't keep it in his pants? Nah, I didn't play by those rules. Content with my decision to piss her off or scare her, I headed toward the rest of the owners to study them. I wanted to learn more to not only become closer to my dad, but also to impress Fern a little bit. Cars were more about colors and brands—either American-made or not.

Larry Fitz sat in a brown and green lawn chair, smoking cigars and watching every person who walked by. I dubbed him the *commander* of the owners and took a chance to talk to him. He proudly boasted that he'd brought four cars to the show and pacified me by answering all my questions. I did bribe him with beer. Thankfully, there were beer tents near the field. I returned with two tall Sam Adams and he pulled out another ugly lawn chair.

"Son, you're telling me you don't know shit about Silvas yet you brought that gorgeous '67? Shit. That's a fucking sin."

"I'm beginning to realize that, Larry." I held up the beer and clinked it to his bottle. "My dad was all about this…shit. Silvas. Engines. History."

"Why ain't you here with him? Huh?" He narrowed his dark eyes, with his large bushy eyebrows coming together like a caterpillar. The image was goofy, but the words were not.

The pinching in my chest came and went, like it had for the past six months, but I swallowed the emotion down. "He passed earlier this year. He wanted to enter his car, talked about it all the damn time, but never got to. Sure, he came to this show summer after summer, but his real love was Rayme."

"Damn shame. Awfully nice of ya to bring her down. Good son." He coughed. He was around the same age as my dad. He even had the same large ears, messy black hair and large middle that wasn't proportional to the rest of his body. "I'm going to finish this beer and tell you the key points for today. We can chat again tomorrow with the second round."

I nodded and leaned into the chair, the hot summer air clashing with the crisp beer in my hands, and for a moment, I understood the thrill. Even talking with the guys in the vendor lot the previous day had entertained me unlike anything I'd done before. The smell of stale smoke, the blistering sun, the laughter... The entire experience had been different. But it was different in a way that called to me. *Why didn't I give it a chance when he was alive?*

"Now, the '67 had significantly fewer models produced that year, way fewer than the prior and following years so that made your beauty rare. That fiberglass sports car also has rocker panels — the lowest body panels on the sides of the car located between the two wheels — and the '67s were given a flat finish without any ribbing."

I frowned and squinted toward Rayme, hoping to spot these rocker panels, and Larry scoffed. "It's the side, yeah?"

"Between the wheels, the low part. Don't call it a side." He shook his head and me and pointed toward the panel I called a side. "Those give the car a lower, smoother outward appearance. Plus, son, you got a good year. That model has a single backup light over the license plate which is specific to '67."

"Good to know, thanks, man." His knowledge about the year and make impressed me. He couldn't pay me to remember all that, but I understood the passion. If he wanted to ask me about cyber security, I could talk for two hours straight without taking a breath. "Say, Larry, how did you get involved with cars?"

He coughed, the sound nauseating me a bit before he spoke. "My dad taught me, then I taught my three sons. They normally come with me, but they got kids and shit now. That's okay, though. Silvas were my first love and likely my last."

"Yeah, my dad was that way too."

"Silvas are a way of life, son. They don't cheat you, leave you, demand things from you. They shine and rumble, the curves smooth and nice." His eyes had a faraway look in them. "I ain't speaking for your father now, but a man has his vice. Having a 'Va as one ain't that bad. Now, I need to finish this cigar and I don't like talking when I smoke. Ruins the experience."

I downed the rest of my beer, laughing at his impatience, and held out my hand to my new friend. "Thanks for explaining. I'll see you later."

"Sure, what's your name anyway?" He wiped his palm on the side of his shorts and shook my hand, his grip a little aggressive and rough.

"Rylan Cirula."

"No shit. Vaughn's kid? I'll be damned. Good man. Proud as hell of you." He clapped my back and let out a whistle. "He passed? I'm so sorry. I never heard. Well, it's good to meet ya. I'll see you around."

Curiosity and shame consumed me. *Larry knew my dad and he was proud of me?* What the fuck—that was a plot twist and the dull thud began again behind my ears. I stretched, hoping to get out the knots, but nothing happened, and I walked around from the judging field with a new resolve. I had to come to terms with the fact that I hadn't given my dad the time or energy for his interests because they didn't fit into my world.

He hadn't put any energy or time into mine, either. It was a two-way street and while there was nothing that could be done to change the past, I could make an effort to learn for the future. I pinched the bridge of my nose, a longing for *something* taking root in my chest and spreading down my limbs. *Sadness? Guilt?*

Hunger?

I knew what it was…the acceptance of my wrongdoing. Silvas weren't my thing but at least I was beginning to understand them. It didn't sit well with me, knowing my error in my father's and my fucked-up relationship, and I busied myself with work until Fern found me a couple of hours later. Her grinning face was about the best thing I had seen in a good long time.

"Is the marijuana, er, I mean, grass issue fixed?" I shoved my laptop into my bag and got up to meet her. I tugged on the end of her hair—her wild blonde locks hung in loose curls, framing her petite tan face. Her cute nose was lined with new freckles and her cheeks had a little burn to them, bringing out the lighter shades of blue in her eyes.

She grinned and rolled her baby blues. "Yes. Thanks again for your help earlier."

"Of course. Now...you promised me a good time. Come on, Big Cheese. Show me the merch and the good stuff." I wanted to grab her hand, protect her for even a little bit, but I froze. She wouldn't appreciate it and the guilt of harboring the secret was already eating at my gut. *To tell her, or to not? How does one start that conversation?*

She ran her tongue over her bottom lip and winked at me. "Merch it is, Moneybags. I can see you now, all decked out in Silvas gear. Tell me, you've seen *Friends*, right?"

"I do live in America."

"I'm going to assume that weird answer was yes, but, the episode with Joey and the Porsche? That's how I'm envisioning you—all decked out in gear you know nothing about." She nudged me with her hip and dared me to argue. I wouldn't, not when she looked like that.

"Excuse me, sassy, but I learned quite a bit about Silvas today."

"Enlighten me, Ry." Her eyes danced with humor and I grew a strong appreciation for the laugh lines around her eyes. She laughed and smiled a lot, and happiness was an attractive trait. So was confidence. Hell, everything she did was attractive. "What did you learn?"

"My car has a single light on the license plate. One of the only models to have it." I puffed out my chest and added a little pep to my gait. "So there."

"Wow, so cool," she replied with clear mockery. "Tell me something I don't know."

I bit the inside of my cheek at her adorable attitude and slung my arm around her. I tucked her right into the crook below my shoulder and held her tight. She fought it for a second, but then relaxed into me. "For being the Big Cheese, I would've thought you'd be a bit nicer. My initial impression of you is shot to hell."

She pinched my side, causing me to squeal, and I flushed with embarrassment. I sounded like a thirteen-year-old girl seeing One Direction. Fern lost her shit, and I mean *lost* her shit. She snorted so hard she leaned over with her hands on her knees. "Holy shit. That sound. I can't breathe."

It went on for a solid five minutes and I was torn between amusement and discomfiture, but her snorting made up for it. She wiped her eyes and reached out to pinch me again, but I jumped a foot away from her. "Hey, now. No way."

"You're ticklish. Like, fucking stupid ticklish. I'm so glad I learned this. I'm going to have a lot of fun with this the rest of the week." She slid her arm around me, not quite putting pressure on the sensitive spot that made me turn into an idiot, but still threatened me. "Trust me, Ry. I'm not going to hurt you. Yet."

I rolled my eyes this time and cleared my throat. Her nostrils flared three times—she was clearly trying not to laugh, and I found it endearing. Not many laughed at me, but she had no problem doing it. It was humbling and refreshing. "We were going to the shop, yes?"

"Right." She led us to the team shop, pushing away from me when we were more in the middle of the show. We couldn't go ten steps without someone saying hi to her or asking a question. It was surreal. My normal day involved me being the celebrity and, for once, I enjoyed not being in the spotlight. It was all her and her yellow hair and big smile.

A large trailer stood off to the right and we walked in, the cool air blasting us the second we entered. Polos of every goddamn color with the Silvas logo on the breast pocket lined the wall. They were not well designed and she kept picking ridiculous options for me to buy. Like the glittery tank-top, the shirt that had two cartoon women in bikinis, or one that said *wrap your ass in fiberglass, drive a Silvas.* "You'd look great in these, handsome. We could rip off the sleeves and make it a muscle shirt. Show off those biceps to all the ladies." She wiggled her eyebrows up and down.

"If I wear that, then you have to wear…hm." I scanned the women's section and found a bikini with Silvas all over it. It was tacky, but small, and my dick liked the thought of Fern in a tiny string two-piece. "This. I wear the muscle shirt, you wear the string."

"Try again." She walked past him and gave my ass a little squeeze. It was so unlike her in her work polo and radio, looking all official, and the gesture had me grinning like an idiot. "What's your style, Ry? I can picture you in jeans and a grungy band shirt but can also picture you all jazzed up in a suit. You look sexy in my head regardless of your outfit, but we gotta get you some shirts to take back."

She fingered the windbreakers and pulled out a navy one with a subtle logo on the sleeve. "Try this one on. It'll look good with your wide shoulders."

I tried her suggestion and surprisingly liked it. It was loose but also stylish enough for me to wear on Fridays at the office. There were a couple of rules I'd bend at work, but work attire was not one of them. Our brand was professional, efficient and consistent. The attire matched that regardless of how much my partner bitched about wanting to wear jeans. "Nice call. I'll get it, but can you help me pick something out for my sister and her spawn?"

"Boys, you said?" She grinned and headed toward the back shelf where hundreds of little Hot Wheels-sized Silvas stood. She grabbed a handful of them, running them over her palm, making engine sounds. "Blue? Yellow? Jungle green — which is my favorite color, by the way — or maybe a black?"

"Doesn't matter. I'll get them all." Analisa's boys loved all things cars, monkeys and lizards. They were my favorite kids on the earth, but they were oddballs. The oldest — Peter — used to play with a turkey baster instead of the hundreds of toys we had bought him. He carried that thing around like a goddamn dog for two years. Again, her kids were weird. "Analisa is about your age, maybe a year older. Any suggestions?"

"Mom, you said? Then a T-shirt that won't be weird to get dirty. My cousin has a bunch of kids and always has a stain on her. Or food in her hair. Hell, kids are gross." She shrugged and pointed to the sale rack. "Puppies I get. They have appeal. But little mini humans? Nah."

"You don't want kids?" *What the fuck did I ask?* "I mean, you're a woman."

Her eyes flared and I closed my eyes, wishing to erase the past five seconds. I held up a hand and put it on her shoulder, pleading with her to let me explain myself. "Fern, forgive me. I tried to backtrack because mentioning kids seemed a little too personal for our five-day relationship. I said the wrong thing, obviously."

She cracked her knuckles, her teeth biting down on her bottom lip for a couple of seconds before she nodded. "I appreciate your honesty, even though your female comment got me all hot and ready to fight to the death."

"Yes. I saw that. My worst moment with you. Won't happen again," I replied while discreetly intertwining our hands behind the clothing rack. I ignored how well her hand fit into mine, because that detail didn't matter. "I want to enjoy every second with you the rest of the week. If I have to stop talking for that to happen, then I'll shut the fuck up."

Her lips quirked up and I swore she leaned into me a bit before bringing her gaze straight to my dick. "I'll remember that if I have to…silence you."

"Kinky. Smart. Beautiful. What can't you do?"

She liked my compliment, going by her warm expression and the straightening of her posture. I was glad I'd said it. She released our grip and pointed to the cashier with a firm expression. "Despite your sexist and dumbass comment, I like you. I'll let you use my employee discount."

"Absolutely not," I yelled. I regretted it the second I said it. Her expression fell, the guard coming back into her eyes, and I rubbed the back of my neck. "No, what I meant to say was thank you. That's kind of you. You're amazing and kind, on top of all the other stuff. I can go on later if needed."

"Definitely needed. But I'll pretend you didn't make an ass out of yourself this little trip and let this slide. That's two strikes though, Ry. Third strike…you'll get it. That's a fucking promise."

"Mm. Don't threatened me with a punishment I want." I winked at her and took all the items up to the counter. She stood close to me, our arms touching, when she told the cashier to use her discount. It was stupid — I had enough money to pay twice the amount, but Fern glared when I even hesitated handing over my card. She gave me a condescending pat on the back when the fifty-percent discount allotted to a very cheap price.

But I kept my mouth shut and thanked her when we got outside. Her reaction was not what I expected at all. An eye roll, a bit of attitude, a comment, sure. But she threw her head back, laughing, and pointed her finger at me. "You are more than just a smart, rich brain. You're good looking, a little playful and great at following directions. You're my kind of man, Moneybags."

Fuck her rules. I cupped her face and kissed her — right in the center of the show. I had to. Her cute expression had so much joy I wanted to be a part of it for a second. And her words... She saw me. She got me. I needed to taste her. She relaxed into it, giving me a slight opening to slide my tongue inside her mouth, but it didn't last long. She tensed and jumped back, her eyes twice their normal size.

"What are you — Rylan. We're at *the show*!" she said with her teeth clenched. The lust that had been in her eyes the second before was gone and instead anger directed at me took its place. "People could see us and you know my thoughts on that."

I put my hand on her shoulder, ignoring the pulse racing at the base of her neck and the faint outline of her hardened nipples, and tried to get her to calm down. I glanced around, not finding one person giving us a weird look. "No one saw, Fern."

"Why—why did you do that?" She ran her fingers over her bottom lip, a dazed expression on her face.

"I just did," I said. She didn't like my answer and I took a step back, lowering my voice. "I'll be on better behavior the rest of the day, but tonight, I will absolutely not."

Chapter Eleven

Fern

Hours later, clean and showered, I was about to write a pro and con list about Rylan Cirula. The confident, sexy man checked every box I could imagine, specifically for our five-day sex-fest. Even the babies comment was forgivable with his awkward regret. I shook my head. I did *not* want to think about Rylan babies, despite how adorable his kids would look. Would they have his dark hair? His soulful eyes and playful spirit?

What the fuck? I shook the thoughts out of my head, going so far as to shake my hair out of my ponytail.

The ball had been in my court the entire week, but I'd trusted him. And for some reason, it seemed important he know it — that was my rationale for dialing his room number with my heart racing. He answered on the third ring.

"Hello?"

"Mr. Cirula? You're needed in room three hundred," I replied in a husky voice and hung up. I'd given him the bait, now he had to take it. I just hadn't considered how brutal the wait time would be. Dressed in a flimsy black lace romper, I had two glasses of Makers on ice waiting for us on the porch. The weather had cooled down a bit since the afternoon and I'd gotten lucky with the view from my balcony. It overlooked downtown St. Louis, the city lights a pleasant view. This city had been my home for almost ten years and it would forever be a part of me. *Unless I get fired...which seems more and more likely.*

I succumbed to the fact that I needed a plan and Mr. Moneybags knew how to create a company — the article he'd been featured in in Chicago might've been open on my phone. He was fascinating, intelligent and down-to-earth for a millionaire. But that wasn't why we had our arrangement. Sex, four orgasms and fun. He was my beautiful distraction from what might very well be my last Silvas show. *Fuck it.* I downed the whiskey, not even enjoying the woodsy taste, and refilled my glass.

Rationally, we should've exchanged numbers, but that would have crossed the invisible line we'd drawn. *Five days. Sex. Fun.* Phone numbers didn't have a place in that formula.

Ten minutes had gone by since I'd called him and my room remained empty. Disappointment, worry and regret were running through me when a loud knock came at the door. *Thank god.*

In eight frantic steps, I stood in front of the beige door and opened it to find Rylan there. A bemused expression on his handsome face, he slid his gaze from my head to my cleavage, then all the way down my bare legs. "Big Cheese, you look delectable."

"Come on in, handsome. Figured it was time you stopped by." I motioned him into the room and admired the way his clothes fit him. A tight black shirt showcased his muscles, his low-riding jeans completing the look. He looked like a normal guy meeting a woman for a drink and nothing like the article I'd read. It pleased me how laidback he was and my relief and happiness at seeing him were genuine. "You had me worried for a bit. I wasn't sure you'd come."

"Oh, I'll *come* tonight for sure. So will you. Four times, if I'm to be exact." He lowered his voice and pulled me flush against him. "I can't get you out of my mind, Fern."

"Your words are like a straight shot of whiskey. Exciting, tasty and dangerous."

He liked that answer—he liked it a whole lot. He grabbed my chin and brought my mouth to his, our tongues greeting each other with a controlled desire. I moaned into his mouth but gently put my hand on his chest. He stilled instantly, giving me a worried look and a slight pout of his wet lips.

His expression made me giggle and I used my thumb to wipe the moisture from his mouth. "Don't give me that wounded look. I wanted to talk to you about something, actually. Thought I'd warm you up with a whiskey first."

"Hm," he responded but searched the room before relaxing. "I'll abide by your rules for a bit, but it's been real hard behaving the entire day. I'd like to be rewarded."

"It could be arranged. Now, come on, handsome."

I handed him the glass and swayed my hips more than normal walking toward the balcony. There were walls on both sides of it, but it overlooked the city and if someone tried hard enough, they could see us out there. The thought sent a thrill through me with what I wanted to do to Rylan. His light footsteps echoed off the tile as soon as he got outside and he chose the chair closest to the wall.

"How did you get a balcony? This is a nice view, even though I hate this city."

"No one hates St. Louis," I scoffed, but he gave me a pointed stare. "Really? Why?"

"Their sport teams. Their fans. The arch. Not a fan of any of it. I'm a fan of you, but please tell me you aren't from here?" He winced when I nodded, but then he reached out and squeezed my knee. "Tough break, Fern. I'll forgive you for it."

"Thank god. I would've lost sleep," I deadpanned. His expression heated over and I realized the double meaning of my words. "I plan to lose sleep with your naked body tonight, don't worry."

"Good. Now, what did you want to talk about? All my blood is going to my cock with you looking like a goddamn angel over there with the lace. *Jesus*, Fern. So, talk real fast."

I chuckled softly and waited until he brought his gaze to mine. "I think I'd like to talk business with you."

His expression fell, the heated eyes becoming clouded, and he looked away from me. It felt like a punch to the gut, like I'd crossed a line and I leaned farther back into my chair to backtrack. "Ry, I know I was an asshole when you talked about it before, but I'm so passionate about the job and the thought of them trying to fire me shocked me, you know? You said something the other day that got me thinking—running my own show. It's terrifying, but you're clearly a good leader and I want to learn from you, if you'll teach me. No pressure. You can say no." My rushed voice sounded desperate, and I bit the hell out of my hangnail.

Every muscle in my body tensed when I waited, scanning his face. Something seemed different. He still looked gorgeous—his hazel eyes lighting up with amusement, but something was off...maybe his posture? The laugh lines around his eyes weren't there. Forgoing my normal boundary, I reached out and traced the lines next to his eyes. "Are you okay?"

He shielded his gaze for two seconds, my stomach tightening in dread. *Does he want to stop this?* Then he smiled, his expression warming as he took my fingers in his hands. "I'm exactly where I want to be."

Damn, I shivered at his words. His grin widened at my reaction and he pulled me into his lap, pressing my back against his chest. He trailed his fingers lightly down my neck, his warm breath hitting my exposed skin and causing my nipples to harden. While the romper left little to the imagination, it wasn't easy to take off. But that didn't stop Rylan.

"I have a confession, Fern. Whenever I'm around you, I have these uncontrollable urges to pleasure you in every possible way. Like right now, I want you to spread your legs wide enough for me. I want you forget everything but me and our bodies. Do you think you can do that for me?"

"Outside?" My voice squeaked, my body warming in anticipation as he brought his fingers up my legs. I bucked when he teased the sensitive skin there, my pulse pounding against my clit. "*Fuck.*"

"You amaze me, and while your body is smoking, I'm talking about *you*. You work so hard and make everyone else happy. Who makes you happy, sweetheart?"

Sweetheart. I clenched my eyes shut, focusing on the long lines he drew on the most sensitive part of my inner thigh. He was being ruthless, going up just close enough to where I needed release, but snatching the sensation away just before I got it. "Don't stop, Ry."

"Answer me, then I'll continue. Who makes you happy?" He trailed his tongue over the edge of my ear, gently pressing his teeth into the delicate skin. His touch was like electricity, spreading too hot and too fast, the speed of my desire out of my control.

"I-I do," I mumbled when he slowly traced the outline of my hardened nipples. He was the master of teasing—tickles and touches that didn't get the job done but fucking got me so hot I would've agreed to anything he asked. "Ry, I'm desperate."

"What are you desperate for? I haven't done anything, really. You're still clothed." He pressed his lips to my neck, biting down just above my collarbone, and it wasn't a delicate bite. "God, I'm not possessive, but I like leaving a mark on you."

"Everything you do feels amazing. But I'm about to go back in there and finger myself if you don't make a move, Casanova," I about screamed. He chuckled in my ear but made no hurried moves. "*Ry.*"

"It's worth the wait, trust me." He brought his fingers toward my center, sliding inside my romper, but continued to tease my folds. "So wet, so hot. I can't tell you how much I love knowing this is for me. Just me."

"God, yes. It's all you." I squirmed against him, his hard cock pressing into me. He hissed when I backed into him more, but he didn't hurry. He took his time, much like how I imagined he did most things in his life. I released a pent-up moan and that finally got him to make a move. He slid his fingers inside me, using his other hand to hold me tighter against him. The combination of pressure built a fiery burn in my core. It wanted an escape, but he wouldn't allow it. He ran his nose down my neck, humming in pleasure, and my entire body shook with need.

"You smell amazing, all the fucking time. I don't get it," he said into my neck, increasing the thrusts of his fingers. He brought his thumb to my clit, swirling around at a rapid pace for ten seconds, then slowing down. "I'm being selfish…I want all of your pleasure."

I shivered at his words, my entire body rigid, ready to burst. I had never experienced lust like this—all-consuming. I turned my face, begging him for a kiss, and he obliged. Our mouths clashed this time, our tongues not able to touch enough or at the pace I craved. I sucked him into my mouth, arching my back when he gave me the release I needed. "Ry, oh my god, yes!"

"Say my name again," he commanded and my body surrendered to him. He had full control of my orgasms and it was fine by me. I rode the high, the burst of adrenaline and ecstasy coursing through my body as wave after wave almost made me lose consciousness. "Say it, Fern."

"*Rylan*, yes."

"Good. Now, turn around."

He hadn't spoken like this before, with the commanding tone and the restraint he barely held on to. I obeyed, desperate and curious to see where it was going. Rylan had let me lead up until this point, and he deserved the chance to have his fun. I got up with shaky legs and this time straddled him face-to-face. He grinned, his broad chest heaving. The only noise between us was our panting breaths and the traffic of the city behind us. He groaned, the sound coming from his chest, and it was deep and intoxicating. "I want to fuck you right here, just like this. Your body straddling me."

I licked my lips. His grin widened and it was a frantic race to undo his belt and slip off his jeans. "Condom?"

"On it." He reached into his pocket and tore it open just as his cock sprang free from my rapid undoing of his pants. He slipped the condom on with such efficiency I didn't have time to react when he lifted me up and set me back down, his cock waiting to enter. "Your clothes?"

"On it," I replied with a wink. I slid the material over to the side and lowered myself onto him, his shaft easing into me like it belonged there. "Fuck yeah, Ry."

He held on to my hips and began thrusting into me, hard. His face...the determined jaw, the burning desire in his eyes and the total lack of restraint would forever be burned in my mind. My romper still being on added desire, the silky material tickling our skin. "Ride me, Fern."

And I did. I rode him, gripping his shoulders while I rocked up and down, letting him fill me to the point of pain, my walls not used to being stretched this way. Sweat collected on his forehead and my attraction to him shattered all expectations. I needed to be closer to him, feel him more. I leaned into him, rocking my hips at a different angle, and he groaned into my mouth.

Our combined moans echoed around us, the sweet humid air making it hard to breathe, and I lost a little piece of my heart. He brought his fingers to my swollen clit and with the combination of his thrusts and varied pressure, my second orgasm took almost no time. He swallowed my moans, humming in pleasure as I cried out his name.

"Amazing," he whispered before gripping me harder. He didn't hold back and the slow burn of him hitting my G-spot was almost too much. I jumped, but he slowed down, finding the perfect pace. We remained like that, together, in sync, and I wanted it to never end. He tensed, his tight muscles tensing as he let out a deep groan, and I decided it was my new favorite sound. Rylan orgasming was an experience. He put his entire body and soul into it, and I was thankful I got to be a part of it...even if only for a short time.

"Jesus Christ." He had a wild look in his eyes, his flushed face a little slack. He kissed my bare shoulder, his touch this time soft and sweet, before staring into my eyes. "You're incredible."

"You too," I replied not able to hold back my huge grin. It was stupid, to feel this giddy. But I did. "I've had more public sex with you the past three days than in my entire life. I gotta say, I'm a big fan."

His eyes darkened for a second, a rare expression crossing his face, before he slowly formed a cocky grin. "I do what I can."

"Oh, shut up." I slid off him and adjusted the romper. While it wasn't exactly lingerie, I was beyond glad I'd brought it to the show this year. Rylan cleaned himself up but left the top button of his jeans undone. It was a goddamn beautiful sight. He caught me staring and smirked at me. I shrugged and replied without shame, "I like looking at you."

"Ditto." He bit down on his bottom lip as his eyebrows came together, his expression a mixture of worry and confusion. "Shit, Fern. I'm sorry."

"Whatever for? I know I've still got two more orgasms later that I'll damn sure cash in."

"No, not that." He rubbed the back of his neck, but then his eyes lit up. "Well, actually, I'll make sure to stay true to my word. But I feel bad. You wanted to talk about business with me and I had my own agenda."

"Ry...do you see me complaining?" I walked up to him with the glasses of whiskey and pressed a kiss on his cheek. His expression changed to shock, and regret shot through me. *Why did I do that? Shit.* I needed to defuse the situation, move it away from sweet to what we planned. *Sex and a little business.* "I couldn't focus on business without a few big Os, so we're good. Now, drink this whiskey, Moneybags, and help a girl out, huh?"

Chapter Twelve

Rylan

She had a fucking clipboard and chewed on the end of her pen. Her legs curled up underneath her shouldn't have had my heart skipping a goddamn beat, but it did. And each time I admired her, both her body and brain, a wave of guilt almost had me excusing myself. *To tell her, or not to?*

"Ry, your eyes have glazed over and we haven't even started," she scoffed. "I guess my body just made you lose your mind. I get it. Happens all the time."

I snapped my gaze to hers, not liking the reference to her past lovers. It was childish and immature, but, fuck, I liked being the *only* one giving her pleasure this week. I waved my hand, dismissing the thought of other men in her life, and leaned toward her, putting my elbows on my knees. "Your body will remain in my mind for years after this, so while your statement was a little bit sassy, it's also true. And I'm sorry. I promise I'm all here. What is your first question, Big Cheese?"

She grinned, a little blush forming on the top of her high cheekbones, and clicked her tongue. "I looked you up. Not creepy stuff, just about your success at your cyber security company. You're quite a businessman, Moneybags."

"Thank you." *Goddamn it, she was looking me up?* It mollified my ego and I fought a grin. "Tell me, did you look at pictures of me and touch yourself?"

"Ha! No, not when I have access to you anytime I want here," she fired back. By god, her words lit me up inside, but I ignored the attraction. She deserved my time, even if we weren't naked.

"That you do. Any time. Any place. Sorry to interrupt. Carry on, BC." I made a circular motion with my hand, trying to mimic a butler's deference, but it didn't work. She just snorted.

"Okay, weirdo, I'm not sure what my goal is yet. I'm going to be honest about that, but I think you're right about getting fired. They are blaming me for things beyond my control—total bullshit move, but it's the truth." She pushed her hair behind her ears when her entire body deflated at her admission. From what I knew of her, this killed her to profess. All her hard work was being disregarded because of Andrew's dick. The ball of guilt formed in my stomach and grew with each word she said. *Fuck. Fucking hell.*

"I think you should start your own Silvas show. Cruising Silvas is a godawful name."

"I know, right?" She grinned but it didn't last long. She bit the pen again and stared at me for a good twenty seconds. "I've always had the idea in the back of my mind, just out of reach. Do you really mean that?"

"You starting your own business? Yes. A million times yes." I reached out and squeezed her knee, hoping it gave her some comfort. "I've watched you work—not in a creepy way, well, a little bit in a sexual way—but how you interact with people. You lead. A natural leader cannot be bought or trained. It's just you. Tell me, if you asked those guys I saw you with, or the girl who calls you Big Cheese, to work for you, what would they say?"

"They'd come with me," she replied in a small voice. Her normal energy was gone, replaced with the fear and uncertainty. I got it. I had been there once, too. "I don't know where I would get the money to start out. We'd have to find a venue, insurance, security…god. I can't believe I'm thinking about this. This is insane. Crazy. What if I lost it all? What if I try this and fail? My mom, uh, she wanted to start her own fashion business when I was young. It didn't work, Ry, it was awful."

"First off, you know the ins and outs of every avenue, right? Do you understand the Accreditation and judging process?"

"Of course. I helped Christine out two full years when I began here. Honestly, it's a bit old-school with all the papers and folders. It could all be moved online and god, she doesn't use any social media. Their entire market would grow if they actually put work into their online presence. That's why so many older people enter—the format caters to them—but let's be honest, the future is the younger crowd."

I grinned. She stood up, the fire that had disappeared for a bit returning full force. She was a joy to watch. She glanced at me and narrowed her eyes. I egged her on, enjoying the little fire inside her. "Keep going."

"I'd have to get a starter loan. I'd need a business plan for it to go through—"

"I'll help any way you want. I know my muscles distract you, but I'm pretty damn good at writing proposals and plans."

"Yeah?" She smiled, the grin taking up her entire face to the point I bit my knuckle to prevent myself from laughing.

"I know my strengths and weaknesses, Fern. I'll help you. I believe in you."

Myriad emotions crossed her face. First, she widened her eyes and blinked at me with an odd expression. Then she rolled her eyes. "What are your weaknesses, Ry? I don't believe you have any."

"Woman, please. You. I'm drawn to you—it's fucking ridiculous." I snorted but her intense gaze had me spilling all my secrets. And once I started, I couldn't stop. "My weaknesses are my family, mainly my dad, my friendships outside of work, sticking to premade plans and sometimes I'm an asshole. I'm good with money but am too focused on what could go wrong in the business, so I forget to enjoy the little moments."

"Must be nice to know yourself."

"I'm a thirty-five-year-old man. I'm still learning, but I'm self-aware. Now, stop getting side-tracked." I gave her arm a squeeze. "You need a proposal and a plan for a loan. You clearly have a knack for marketing and social media—how many people would you need working for you, for it to function successfully?"

"Hmm. Good question." She paced again, her bare feet hitting the tile. I didn't have to ask to know very few people saw her like this, her hair down and wild, her eyes a little tired but full of life. It pleased me, just another thing about her that was going to be hard to say goodbye to come the final day. "I've taken on a lot the past couple of years. The only thing I've never done is the graphic design for the branding."

"Get a college kid who needs experience. Shit, that's how I started out. I found four college kids with computer science majors and a little bit of coding experience. They got free internship hours for a year and now two of them work for me."

"That's a great idea. I could model that system with our social media, too. Rich and Karl could handle vendors...Gary could still do the clubs and caravan. Clothing...shit! Kayla!"

"Little Cheese?"

She threw her head back and laughed with a nod. "Yes. I'm using that on her now. I'd name her VP in a heartbeat. She knows everything. I'd have to freshen up on the judging and Accreditation ...but I could do it. I have enough in savings just in case something goes wrong and I know enough contacts in the field to have a baseline of support. I would be successful if I took the right steps."

"I have no doubt."

She clapped three times and took two larges strides toward me. She didn't wait before grabbing my face and planting a wet, sloppy kiss on my lips. "Thank you." *Kiss.* "Thank you so much." *Another kiss.*

It was fucking cute. I picked her up and moved her onto my lap, not unlike our position earlier, but this time I had no intention of fucking her. It was simply because I wanted to hold her. "What's your first step then?"

She scrunched her nose and made the tiniest sound of uncertainty. The cute noise went straight to my chest. "Discreetly make a connection with the judges tomorrow at their dinner."

"The judges get a dinner?"

"Yup. Christine caters to them. Last I remember, these old men are super dramatic and want the world given to them. It also pisses me off there are just *two* women. I don't like that ratio at all."

"You know, I think there were about eight owners who weren't men. But that could be too high of a guess."

"It's annoying. I'm hoping to network tomorrow. It's a big thing. Black tie dinner with a guest speaker and all that. I'm required to go, but I tend to hate it."

"Want me to fake an emergency to get you out of it?" I trailed my fingers up and down her back, her flesh breaking out in goosebumps when I rubbed her. She liked it, I knew, but she didn't know how much I liked her skin. *Smooth, warm, perfect.*

"Ha! I wish. But with my new plan, I need to chat it up with the head judges." She cupped my face this time, her genuine happiness contagious.

"Head judges? Jesus, this is like a reality TV show."

"It's worse," she replied with a snort. "There are five divisions, and each has a head judge. Those are the guys I need to connect with if I want to steal them from Andrew."

"I'm selfish when I want something, and I want you all the time I can get. What time is this shit over?"

She giggled and patted my shoulder. "Calm down, Rambo. It's over at ten. I can try and sneak out around nine. It's downtown at some fancy bar."

"Black tie, you said? You'll be wearing some sexy black dress?"

"It's a bright blue, and while sexy isn't what I go for with a room full of men over sixty, I'd confidently say it hugs my curves nicely."

"Have I mentioned I love your body yet today?" I ran my hand down her side, making sure to graze her breasts and the beautiful curve of her thighs. "I can pick you up?"

"That'd be nice, yeah. I could show you my favorite part of the city."

I grunted. "You're my favorite part of this city."

"Your lines work so well on me now. That first night…they were lame." She tilted her head and pursed those pink lips.

"Excuse me, they were not lame. You came up with me and goddamn, I'm glad you did." I pinched her side and enjoyed her squirming against me. "I liked your audacity and brazenness then, and even more so now."

She didn't respond, just let out a soft sigh. I could picture it—us, sitting like this back in my loft in Chicago. But the thought came and went because that wasn't part of the plan. But then she snuggled deeper into my chest and something unraveled inside me. The insistence on being married to my career, the fear of finding a woman who wanted my wealth, not me, and the pride I had not letting someone have power over me. Because Fern had it, even if she didn't realize it. The thought should've terrified the hell out of me…but it didn't. I kissed her temple, her cute little sigh the perfect reward, and held her tighter. She yawned and I rubbed her arms. "You tired, BC?"

"Exhausted, suddenly."

"Come on, let's go to bed." I picked her up and carried her back into her room. I set her on the bed and went to close the patio door, but her bottom lip came out in the cutest little pout. "What's wrong?"

"Are you leaving?"

"Fuck, no. I'm shutting the door and might beg to use your toothbrush?" I made a goofy smile at her and she relaxed. Her relief caused another squeeze of my heart, the guilt growing more and more. "I'm glad you want me to stay."

"Why wouldn't I?" She chuckled and pulled the blanket up to her neck. "God, is it midnight already? I like talking with you."

Guilt. Regret. Shame.

"We have two more days, Fern. You need rest if you're going to take over the world." I closed the patio door, picked up the glasses of whiskey and dumped them in the bathroom sink. I hated myself in that moment. I knew a secret, one that affected her life, and I hadn't told her out of cowardice, fear and the foolish hope I'd misunderstood what had been said. All the above. But…if she started her own company, it would be better for her. *Right?* I splashed water on my face, disgusted with myself and ashamed I could be hurting a woman I had grown to…care for. I gripped the edge of the counter and did what I did best — I formed a next-steps list.

Helping Fern start her business plan.

Preparing her any way I can.

Enjoying her every second I have left.

Confronting Andrew and forcing him to tell her.

She deserved to hear it from him, not me. It could be a mistake and she had history with her boss. Even though he was a scumbag, he owed her the truth. *Plus, he could change his mind, do the right thing after all. Or maybe Fern won't believe me.* The thought stung, but it was still true. We were still learning each other and it had been less than a week—she'd known her boss for years.

Content with my decision, I joined her in bed after removing my clothes. She still wore her sexy romper, but I could still feel her heat when I pulled her against me. "Goodnight, Fern."

Her voice was clogged with sleep. Her hair was in every direction, but none of that mattered. She rolled closer to me, putting her head on my shoulder, and her breath hit my face. Guilt racked me again at how much I liked her. It worsened after she whispered the words, "I don't even have time for a real relationship because of this job, so how could I bring kids into this world?"

I wasn't sure if she wanted me to answer or listen, and her light snore gave me a clue. Thankful I didn't have to respond, I didn't sleep a wink for the next hour. I just held her in my arms, forcing myself to be content with my plan. I wouldn't hurt Fern…but worry lodged itself in my chest, spreading throughout my body. *What if I do?*

Chapter Thirteen

Fern

Perfume and an extra layer of mascara went a long way — the push-up bra enhanced a bit, too, but while my boobs were naturally perky, my eyelashes were not. I blinked and added one more layer, helping my blue eyes stand out more than normal. It was a requirement for the fancy judges' dinner and about one of three times a year I dolled up. One was always a wedding, the other either a funeral or a charity benefit for Silvas. It was shocking that my life revolved around everyone else in my life…it was never for me.

Knock it off. I squashed my self-deprecating thoughts and focused on the good. There'd been no issues the entire day — not one. Everything had run smoothly and while the high from having a great day had worn thin, the adrenaline from forming my plan had kept me going. *I'm not my mom and I can do this. I will succeed.*

I'd chatted with two judges during the event, with the help of Rylan of course, and had learned more about the process to even become a judge. I could do it. I could run my own show, update a lot of archaic practices and make enough profit to pay the employees who busted their asses.

I straightened my spine, applied a final layer of lipstick and about jumped out of my heels when someone knocked on my door. I peeked through the peephole and couldn't contain my excitement at seeing Rylan there.

"Moneybags, to what do I owe this pleasure?" I opened the door and leaned on the frame, eyeing his sleek black pants and dark gray button-down. He looked like a beautiful sin and a part of me wanted to invite him inside my room and say to hell with the judges' dinner. His eyes heated over, his defined jaw tensing. His gaze started at my feet, worked its way up my skin-tight dress with a deep cutout down the center of my chest, and finally met my eyes.

"Holy shit."

I chuckled and shimmied for him. "Take a picture if you must."

"It wouldn't even do you justice. *Jesus*, woman. You fill out that dress in the best way. Let me see more." His voice got real low and he ran his hand down my cutout, the sensitive skin between my breasts tingling with anticipation.

I spun around, enjoying his slight intake of breath at the low neckline in the back, and might've given him a confident smirk at the end. "I take it you like the dress, no?"

"Uh, yeah. Fuck yeah. So much...I'd prefer you maybe not wear that around a bunch of sixty-year-old men. I know men and, sweetheart, you're lethal." His expression matched the tone of his voice and while it pleased me, I still didn't understand why he was here.

"Not that I don't enjoy seeing you, but I do have to head to the event and I'm on my way out." I sucked my bottom lip into my mouth before giving him a weak smile. "So…watcha doing up here?"

"Being a goddamn gentleman. Well, trying to be. Your dress is making it really difficult. But I came to offer to drive you. I can drop you off and pick you up when you're ready."

"Interesting proposition." My body craved him and my heart was hesitant, but I found myself nodding anyway. "Okay, deal. But how are you going to know when to pick me up when we aren't exchanging numbers?"

"We could change that?" he asked, his voice rising a bit too high. I shook my head and wiggled my finger at him.

"Nope. What's the fun in that?" I grabbed my small purse, leaned into the mirror and made sure everything was in place. Rylan took that opportunity to move in behind me, his head just inches above mine. We looked good together — better than good — and my heart fluttered. His eyes smoldered when he pressed a light kiss on my neck.

"You look beautiful, Fern."

"Th-thank you." My voice broke. It was intense, that moment. It blurred our line, the fun and hook-up one, with something else. It lasted too long, clogging my throat with words I didn't know how to say, then my phone ringing broke the tension. I leapt out of his grasp and read a text from Christine.

Are you on your way? I need you here.

I snuck a glance at Rylan, debating my options. *Fuck the invisible line drawn between us.* I had one more day with him and if he wanted to drive me, then so be it. "Handsome, if you'd still be willing to drive me, I'd appreciate it."

"Offer never left. Let's head there, BC." He held out his arm at an awkward angle, waiting for me to take it, and I chuckled. It was like going to prom with the prom king. "Wait, before we go, I need to do something."

"Wh—" I didn't get to finish. He pushed me up against the door, placing his hands carefully on my neck so as not to mess up my hair, and kissed the hell out of me. It was a desperate kiss, a mixture of saying goodbye and hello at the same time. It pulled at my heartstrings. His minty taste instantly shot a burn of desire through me, and I knew without a doubt I'd miss him. Seconds, maybe minutes, later he pulled back with the sexiest smile I had ever seen. "Wow."

"Ditto your wow. I messed up your lipstick, sorry." He gave me a sheepish look and wiped under my mouth. "This is meant as a compliment, okay? The red lipstick looks great, but I prefer your bare lips. You have a great mouth and it doesn't need any enhancement."

"Thank you," I mumbled shyly. *Fuck.* I wasn't shy when it came to sex or hook-ups. I owned that shit, getting a few orgasms and walking away at the end. But this…this was new territory. "I like getting dressed up about three times a year. This is the second time."

"Wish I could see the other two. Now, let's leave this room before I forget my manners."

He led me down the hall and to the elevator, leaving space between us the entire time. It was torture. But my rules remained in place and while I could fault him for the kiss the day before, he had been perfect every other second. "My car's parked over here. Come on, beautiful."

I wanted to roll my eyes, but it wasn't a line from him. I felt his words in how he looked at me, how he touched me, and fuck...tomorrow was going to be rough. He placed his hand on the lower part of my back — like the first night — and guided me toward the passenger door before opening it for me. "Thank you, sir, I appreciate you."

"Anything for the Big Cheese."

I had twenty seconds to gather my wits before he got into the car with his delicious cologne and cute banter. I took a long breath and reordered my priorities —

Survive the judges' dinner.

Finish the show without issue.

Confront Andrew and/or start my own business.

Rylan didn't fit into that plan, but I wanted him to. Maybe I could fit him in between the show ending and the conversation with Andrew? I didn't get an answer though. He jumped in and winked before pressing a kiss on the back of my hand. I swore I swooned, something I hadn't done in ten years. "Ry, tell me, are you always this chivalrous with the ladies?"

"I should say yes, to show how great I am, but something about you...you have me twisted up. In a good way, of course." He gave me a tight smile, his expression changing from playful to serious in a split second. "Should I be outside at nine?"

"Yup. I'll fake an emergency. A tent issue, if that works for you," I replied, hoping to ease the awkward tension that had somehow snuck into his SUV. We hadn't experienced this level of heaviness and I wanted to go back to the fun, sexy time. "Have you ever had car sex, Ry?"

"Ah, no." He blushed and gave me a quick glance before going onto the highway. "I know this might surprise you, but I was a bit of a nerd growing up. By the time I grew some muscle, I was into my business and it became all about the money."

I frowned, reaching for his leg and giving him a quick pat. "I have a lot of thoughts about your statement. One…I want to pop your car cherry and I promise it'll be worthwhile."

His posture straightened and gone was the rare moment of weakness. He raised his eyebrows and gave me the cockiest grin I had seen on him so far. "Yeah? I'm going to hold you to that."

"I expect nothing less. But, the second thought…you're more than your money. You're more than your company. Fuck those money-grabbers. I'm sure you're quite a catch."

He slid his warm gaze to mine and all sorts of promises swirled in his eyes, but he didn't voice any of them. He just gave me a quick nod and muttered, "Thanks, Fern."

We didn't need to speak the rest of the ride. The comfortable silence didn't bother me. In fact, I relished it. It usually took me months to feel content with someone without having to fill the void in conversation, and with him, this quickly… It'd be easy to wish for more. I didn't worry about false promises or hidden motives with him—he was upfront, something I hadn't found in a man in a good long time. I questioned my plan and wondered how I could fit him in when he pulled up into the swanky restaurant. "Thanks, Moneybags."

"Of course. I'll be here at nine."

I moved to get out of the car, but he grabbed my wrist and pulled me closer to him. "Ry! What are you doing?"

"Reminding you to not get any ideas with all those desirable old men." He gave me a panty-melting, inhibition-forgetting, soul-crushing kiss that wasn't fair. I had to head into a dinner without acting like I was wet and turned on. "Now you can go."

"Asshole," I whispered and earned a chuckle from him. "Try not to think about car sex for the next two hours...or my mouth on your cock."

He sucked in a breath and I closed the door, pleased I'd gotten a reaction from him. Now I just had to survive two hours coddling old guys and two women, and figure out how to get as many of them as I could to join my team. It shouldn't be too difficult.

* * * *

Andrew Rosales charmed the crowd with the perfect speech, thanking Christine and me for our hard work, thanking the judges for their contribution. After all, without them, there wouldn't be a show. I rolled my eyes when he gushed over Marla and her photography. He even pointed out two portraits that were for sale. I didn't correct him when in fact I'd taken one of the pictures. Marla sat at the head table right next to Andrew and Christine, and the sight of them disgusted me. Every year before, the three of us had sat together and laughed, talking about the ups and downs of the show, but we'd known we'd be back the next year. This time was different.

James Mercer approached me with a glass of wine and a kind smile. "You look like you need this."

"I do, thank you." I gave him a weak smile and slunk back to my chair. He was the leader of the judges' union—which wasn't a recognized thing, but if there were one, he'd be in charge. "You enjoying yourself, James?"

"Not as much as previous years, but not the worst. You're working yourself to death, Fern. That's not new…but make sure you take care of yourself. The turnout seems good this year, huh?"

"Best numbers we've had in five years. Listen, I have a question for you. Can I trust you to be discreet?"

"Sure." He furrowed his graying eyebrows and leaned closer to me. I was going with my gut on this one, trusting how I felt around him. He had never been caught up in lying, cheating the system or kissing Christine's ass, and if I could get him to move with me…the rest would follow. I cleared my throat and set the glass down so I wouldn't squeeze it to death.

"If another Silvas show would happen, say in Chicago or Cincinnati or elsewhere, what would it take for you and your guys to make it out there?"

He gave me a long look, one that had me squirming with nerves and regret. *What if he tells Andrew my question?* But then he gave me a nod, almost like approval, and reached into his back pocket. "Let's let the dust settle from this year. Give me a call in three weeks and we can chat about whatever you got going on in your head."

"Thank you, James. I appreciate your discretion," I replied and held out my hand. He shook it and gave me a little wink. Then he left me at the table with a slow bubble of excitement. He hadn't flat-out said what I needed to hear, but it had been the next best thing. Step one, completed. It was close enough to nine to sneak out and it was freeing to not feel guilty for leaving. For too long, I'd stayed out of duty. But no more. I didn't owe Andrew and Christine anything since they hadn't said ten words to me the entire night. Christine either blinked too much when I tried talking to her, or gave me awkward, one-word answers. Andrew...he, too, seemed to be avoiding me. *Two more days...that's all and I can leave.*

I downed the glass of white wine, all my thoughts on Rylan and the crazy things we could do while naked, and waltzed through the foyer until I came into the bar area. The weirdest sensation came over me, something like awareness and excitement all rolled into one. Rylan sat at the bar, a half-drunk whiskey held up against the side of his face, and he stared right at me with his dimpled grin. The back of my neck tingled. My throat burned with emotion. My heart raced and I couldn't stop the gigantic smile from spreading across my face. He downed the drink and moved in a swift motion, taking four steps until he met me. He didn't say a single word. He just held out his hand and I took it.

That was when I realized I would follow him anywhere if he asked me to. It wasn't about losing my independence, or my strength, but more about what we were together. He led me through the exit, a slight breeze meeting us. It reminded me of the summer storm that had hit — causing us to seek shelter in a tent. Suddenly, I needed him.

"Where's your car?"

"A block away. Are you okay?"

"More than okay. Come on, handsome, I've been thinking about you between my legs for two hours. I want to pop your car cherry."

"Goddamn it, woman." He laughed and took off jogging, I followed. *Fuck pleasing my boss and Christine. Fuck worrying about so many other people. It's about me now. Me and Rylan.*

We got to his car. The street around the warehouse district was empty. the only sounds coming from an occasional car on a busy street a block away. He dropped his keys. Twice. "Nervous, Moneybags?"

"Horny, Big Cheese. Never nervous."

"That's awful confident for a guy who has no idea what we're about to do…" He unlocked the back of the SUV and practically threw me into it. I gasped when he covered my body, sliding his hands under my clothes and removing my panties in one motion. "Oh, wow. The nerd got some moves."

"Don't forget it, either."

Thank Christ his SUV had tinted windows. The back seats were still pushed down from hauling the wood and sod, and he lifted my dress up and didn't wait before dropping his mouth down on the most sensitive area of my body. "Rylan, *Jesus.*"

"I don't have too much longer to eat you. I want my fill."

He got his fill, and some more. He tongue-fucked me, slipping in and out of me with the skill of a lover who'd been with me for years. He gripped my waist, pulling my pussy tight against his mouth as he devoured me. He used two fingers, combining the thrusts with his tongue, and all thoughts left me.

Pleasure.

Rylan.

So close... My stomach tightened and he sucked harder, sending me over the edge. I cried out when the first orgasm hit me fast. He was everything, his touch, his scent, his voice, and I lost myself as he licked up evidence of my pleasure.

"You're so fucking beautiful, Fern." His voice was low, gravelly and sent a wave of desire through me.

Bliss took over and I wasn't sure if I opened my eyes. My entire body hummed with an energy I hadn't experienced as he slipped a condom on before entering me, my dress still on and all. "It's never enough with you. I don't get it."

"I know," I mumbled when he filled me, completely and frighteningly. "I *know*."

This time was different. Slower. It was sensual, calm and the burn took its time. At one point, he stopped thrusting and kissed me. His tongue danced with mine. My eyes stung from the overt display of affection and I had to quickly wipe away any evidence of the emotion. He kissed my temple. "You're." Kissed my left eye. "Fucking." Kissed my right eye. "Beautiful."

Then he picked up the pace, making sure my clit got the right angle and pressure, and we fell apart together in the back of an SUV. He held on to me while I trembled around him, gasping for air when the orgasm stole all my breath. He said my name, drawing it out and making it sound like a prayer, when he convulsed on top of me. It was...different. Almost like—

"I've never made love before. Definitely not in the back of a car."

"God, we're on the same page. I just thought that," I admitted.

He grinned down at me, the street lights illuminating his smile. "You're different. In the best way, I mean."

I pushed myself up onto my arms and bit my lip. He blinked a couple of times and I swore he blushed, but I wasn't going to help him out. He slid my panties up my legs, carefully, taking his time. It was sweet.

"Amazing," he said, grabbing my face for a quick kiss.

I grinned into his kiss and fisted his shirt in my hand. "Tell me, Moneybags. How does it feel getting to do it in the back of a car?"

"I'm torn." He smoothed down his hair and gave me a long look. He squinted his dark eyes, a telltale sign he was deep in thought. "While I'm glad I can finally not lose a point when I'm forced to play *never have I ever*, my knees hurt. Does that make me old?"

"Nah, my ass has a little rug burn, too. Battle scars, handsome. Now, let's go back to my room and take a bath in my big-ass tub to…ease the pain."

"Gorgeous and a genius. I love your plan."

I laughed, but his face turned serious, different from any other expression I had seen. He tilted my chin up and ran his thumb over my bottom lip.

"Tomorrow," he said.

"What's tomorrow?"

"We talk about this. Us. What happens when the show is over, because we are *not* done."

Heart racing, brain swirling, thoughts jumbled…I nodded. "Okay."

Chapter Fourteen

Rylan

I want a relationship with Fern. A real one. One beyond the five days we granted ourselves for pleasure and a distraction from something we both craved. The thought of not waking up with her next to me ever again did not sit well with me. She'd worked her way into my stone heart and I didn't want her to leave. *Not for a good long while.*

"Final day of the show. Thank Christ." She stretched, arching her arms above her head and giving me an amazing view of her back. Her muscles tightened and I reached out to trace the lines of her shoulders. She was toned and took care of her body — it turned me on. Even now, after an entire week of fucking her, her bare back got me hot. She hummed, the sound hitting me somewhere near my heart, and I continued massaging the knots. "Mm, that feels good."

"You're stressed already. I thought your orgasms would've helped with all these balls of stress. What's on your mind?"

She continued leaning closer to me and I used both hands to give her a light rub. Her sounds were worth the extra effort. "Last-day jitters. I get a post-event hangover, the millions of things to do switch to about five and I don't know how to handle the downtime. I get anxious."

"Mm, well...I know what we can do tonight to help busy you."

"I'm counting on it, handsome." She turned her head just enough so I could see her grin, and I kissed her spine. Once toward the bottom, again in the middle and a third one at the base of her head. Then I licked up to her neck and gave her a little love bite. *Obsessed.* Goddamn, I was obsessed with her body.

I cleared my throat and forced myself not to lose control that early in the morning. "How does your day look? I'm asking because I care, but also because I want to know when I get to see you again."

She blushed at my words, her nose scrunching just a little bit, and I decided to compliment her every chance I got. Her smile was killer. "Vendor checkout. Deposit returns — if they stayed the entirety of the show, they get a check for a hundred bucks — and the Caravan. But Gary handles the seven-hundred Silvas run, thank god. Then...after-party." She turned all the way around, content in her nudeness, and leaned over to kiss me. "I gotta jet."

I pouted, not giving a shit that I was a grown man. "Fine."

"You're pretty cute when you make that face."

"I'm not cute. Manly, masculine, beefy. Any of those work," I teased and earned another grin. "Sexy, sinful, amazing work, too."

"Nah, I like cute. It's good for your ego." She tickled my side and I let out a yelp. This caused her to go into a fit of giggles, falling onto my lap with each snort. I pulled her closer and if I didn't stop it, I'd ravage her body. I took the mature route.

"No one says that, by the way. *I gotta jet.*" I pursed my lips, getting my third and favorite smile from her. This one reached both her stunning eyes and set warm tingles in my gut.

"I do." She stood, giving me another fantastic view of her curves. "My body has never felt so tight and relaxed at the same time. I blame you."

"Me? I followed through on my four orgasms a day, Fern."

"Oh, I know. But I'm going to walk funny today if I'm not careful." She gave me a cheeky grin and threw on the same attire she'd worn all week — khaki shorts and a yellow polo. "Damn. Leaving you, looking like that in bed, is harder than I thought."

"I've been telling you that all damn week."

She scrunched her nose with a quick smile and threw her hair up into a messy bun. It completed her look. Cute, put together and sexy as hell. Okay, that was my opinion, but it didn't make it not true. "Ten."

"Ten, what?" I asked.

"Meet me outside the offices at ten and we can chat." She wiped under her eyes, giving me another scorching kiss before grabbing her keys. "I don't say this lightly, but I don't think I'm ready to let you go."

"Be still my fucking heart." I grabbed her waist, pulling her toward me and wrapping my arms around her. "Glad we're on the same page. But we kinda have been the whole week, yeah?"

"Agreed, now let me go, handsome, or I'm going to have a shit-storm waiting for me."

I squeezed her one last time, sneaking another long, wet kiss in, and let her go. "I'll meet you at ten."

She breezed out of the room, leaving me in her hotel bed with all her things around me. I had a plan and it wasn't going to get done lounging around for another hour. I got up, showered and dressed before heading to my room. My partner didn't call me ruthless for nothing, and it was about time Andrew got what was coming to him. I stewed the entire drive there, planning the best attack on a man willing to let his dick ruin his business.

Laptop and coffee in hand, I strode onto the field after a quick wave to Kayla. She greeted me at the entrance with the same cute blush and knowing glance. Today was the day of the show, where owners found out their Accreditation, and I didn't have to get into the line-up until noon. They did a whole thing where every owner drove their car or cars through a line where Andrew announced the Accreditation they'd won. There were speakers, photographers, music and the whole nine yards. It felt weird and stupid to win an award for something I had no control over, but the reminder of my dad stopped my negative thoughts. It was for him.

But also a little bit for me, too.

Noon gave me two hours to confront Andrew, two hours to share everything with Fern, and time to hopefully fulfill my dad's wish. It was a lot for me to handle.

I put headphones in, went into the makeshift office Christine had introduced me to the first day and got through about ten emails, all detailing concerns they had about our latest program. I was proud of it—it helped detect an attack or intrusion on a network before it got too late—but I forwarded all the messages to my partner. He could handle it for one more day. Instead, I looked at flights from St. Louis to Chicago...if Fern would let me, I'd fly out the next weekend to see her.

But that was a big *if*, and I didn't like not knowing the outcomes of things. I controlled business conversations and if I didn't like them, I cut off that client. Friends, if they were dicks, I'd cut them from my life. That was the thing with my family. I didn't get along with my Mom that much, but I knew how all conversations would end, the guilt and awkward tension every single time. I could prepare for it. Talking with Fern would be an entire new area for me and while the thought of continuing our relationship excited me, it had me sweating.

But first, Andrew Rosales, CEO and asshole. I researched a bit about him and while I didn't find anything alarming, he hadn't updated the website, their programs or requirements for seven years. *Good God, that's the kiss of death in business.* The website looked like trash and, after digging a little deeper, it seemed odd how he owned two residences in different states. From what Fern said, the company didn't make a high profit... Despite how hard she worked, it didn't seem like she was getting compensated for it. *Another thing about running a business—paying employees what they're worth.* Andrew was shady and it sure as fuck didn't sit well with me. I outlined in my mind how I wanted to talk to him, but fate had other ideas. The door opened and his recognizable gravelly voice carried over the small wall. It appeared Marla was with him and suddenly, my plan shifted. He handed me the conversation on a silver platter.

"God, yes, baby. I wanted to get my fill of you before my husband gets here. You're so sexy, Drewy."

Drewy? I gagged and calmed my rising temper.

The CEO laughed and a loud smacking sound echoed off the walls. Marla cooed, "I love it when you spank me. Yes. Do it again!"

The sound happened three more times before something crashed onto the ground. I assumed they were too busy with each other, and snuck a glance behind the corner. They were making out like two uncontrollable teenagers, Marla's ring glistening in the sunlight from the window, and my disgust grew.

"Baby, you're not going to fire my mom, are you?"

The goddamn sneak. She pouted, dragging her fingers up and down his body as her unbuttoned shirt left her tits on display. It was a part of her plan to blackmail him. He was a fool. His gaze was only on her massive tits when he shook his head. "Of course not, sexy. I wouldn't do anything to mess this up."

"Good. Now, I need to take some photos, or someone'll get suspicious. I'll find you later and give you that blowie you wanted." She giggled when she spoke and he ate it up. She redid her shirt, jumped onto his waist and kissed him. I'd recognized her tactics within five seconds. The young, attractive married woman wanting to ensnare her mom's boss...but it contradicted Christine's conversation with Andrew. Unless Christine was in on it too... *Christ.* I rubbed my temples and waited until Marla left the office.

The second the door closed, I let all my feelings turn off. This was about Fern and what was right. He stood there, hopelessly watching Marla waltz around outside with men walking up to her the second she appeared.

"We need to talk. Now." I used the voice often called ruthless in business meetings. He clutched his chest and spun around so fast he fell to the ground. My lip curled in disgust and I wasn't about to offer to help him. "You have five seconds to right yourself."

"M-Mr. Cirula, uh, what—it's not what—"

"Stop your blabbering. Christine kindly offered me this back cubicle to work in during the week. This is not the first conversation I've overheard. Care to take a guess what else I heard? I dare you."

His face went from a fiery red to a pale white, his eyes glossing over as he wiped his forehead. He plopped down into the plastic chair, his weight causing it to creak with the pressure. He put his head in his hands and let out a long, ragged sigh. "Fuck. Fuck! This isn't good."

"Nope. Really not good. Let me get this straight. Feel free to fill in any gaps I might have. And if you think for one second I'm not going to report your ass, guess again." I stepped toward the small black table and enjoyed his misery. "You're hooking up with Marla—Christine's daughter. Marla won't let you fire her mom because she's got your dick whipped, and Christine won't let you fire her or she'll report you."

"What have I done?"

"I don't really care. You made your choices. Am I off, or missing anything?"

"No. No. It's… I— Marla and I are going to be together."

"You naïve man. She's using you, but I'll let you find that out on your own. Now, I'm going to tell you what you're going to do."

"Excuse me?" He fired up, anger burning in his eyes. I welcomed the challenge and placed the palms of my hands on the table, lowering my head toward him.

"I'm going to tell you what you're going to do for two reasons. One, you owe it to Fern, the collateral damage in your fucked-up life. Two, if you don't, I'm worth more than you'll ever be and I'll buy out the company, fire your ass and blacken your name so no one in their right mind will hire you. You're going to tell her, then give her the company or you'll see this place die. Am I clear or do I need to re-explain myself?"

"Why the fuck do you care?" He stood up and gripped the back of his chair, a vein in his forehead bulging. "How dare you come in here, threaten me and my company? Buy me out? As if. It would be at least three million and I'm not sure you could—"

"I make that much in a month. Try me, Andrew Rosales." I hated using my wealth. I detested anyone who used it as weight to gain power, but this guy and his unfair treatment pushed every fucking one of my buttons. My blood rushed to my ears, the sound roaring while I controlled my anger. A breeze hit my face, but I didn't care—all I wanted to do was punch this guy's face. "God, it pisses me off to no end you telling Fern she has to raise revenue by five percent. You damn well know the only way that would happen would be with you and Christine. Rule number one about running a company, don't fucking sleep with anyone there."

"I see you're real acquainted with Fern, huh?" He grinned and walked behind me, forcing me to turn and face him. I wouldn't put it past him to sucker-punch me. "Sleeping with her, I presume? Interesting. See, she signed a contract saying that was a fireable offense."

"Good for her. You sure as hell didn't give a flying fuck when you started banging Marla."

"I didn't sign that contract. I'm the CEO." He puffed his chest and his gaze slid to the right of me for a split second, but his words and ego distracted me. "I can ask around, see if anyone saw you two together. It would be easy grounds for dismissal."

"While I'm sure you'd love to find anything to help your argument, none of this is your business." I crossed my arms and planned my next attack. "However, you fucking Christine's daughter and Christine blackmailing you to fire Fern *is* her business."

Someone gasped, a glass shattering behind me. I jumped and turned to see Fern standing there, slack-jawed and wide-eyed. She blinked five times before her lip trembled, the pain on her face so evident that my throat hurt. "Fern," I said, but she looked away.

She straightened her posture, a mask forming on her face. I recognized the battle stance, and while my heart hurt for her, she needed to deal with this on her own terms. She slowly pointed her finger between Andrew and me, her lip curling up in revulsion. With a shaky voice she said, "Is this true? Everything I heard."

"Yes." I took a step toward her, desperate to comfort her but not having a single clue how to help. The ball of dread burst inside my stomach and the only thing I could do was tell the truth. "I don't know what you heard, but Andrew has been sleeping with Marla for some time and Christine knows. He threatened to fire her if she told you, and Marla is using sex to keep her mom's job. They were going to push you out because your boss couldn't keep his dick to himself. I'm so sorry."

Her gaze went to Andrew, her pale blue eyes dimming, but she brought it back to me and deflated. Her posture caved, all the confident energy I had grown to lo—appreciate gone. "You *knew* this? This whole time?" Her voice broke, the sound like a knife to the gut. She blinked and pressed her lips together so hard they turned white. "Even after...our conversations about the future...you didn't tell me?"

"You deserved to hear it from him, not me." While it didn't make this situation any easier, it made the most sense. I just prayed she understood that.

She sucked in one side of her cheek, not giving one glance at Andrew. Tension built in my lungs, as if someone was pressing down on my ribcage with a weight. She shook her head, clenching her fist before narrowing her eyes at me. "Fuck this. I don't need this shit. Not today, not right now."

Then she left the room, Andrew trying to sneak out behind her. I snapped. "Where the *fuck* do you think you're going? We're not done, you piece of shit. I was being polite before. But you hurt Fern, *again*, and that's just unacceptable."

Chapter Fifteen

Fern

Whiskey.

It had helped me through my first break-up in college, the broken engagement at twenty-two, and now…the five-day sex-fest with an amazing guy. *Only, he turned out to be a liar…right?* That was why I was mad. He'd known, had his way with me and kept that secret. I scoffed, grabbed the glass bottle and headed off out of sight for a while. My sunglasses blocked my face — probably a good thing since my eyes gave every emotion away — and I ignored the waves and the questions on people's faces. *Not today, people. Not right now.*

Ten minutes later, after I snuck past the other workers and vendors who always needed *something*, I slowed the golf cart and said to hell with it. I took a swig of the whiskey reserved for the after-party, damned well knowing no one would care if I returned with a slightly woodsy scent to my breath. The liquid burned my throat, my nose stinging along with my eyes, but it was a good kind of pain. It helped the raging battle going on in my head and heart. *Ugh.*

"Big Cheese, you there?" Kayla's voice crackled over the radio. *Damn it. I should've silenced it as soon as I walked out of the office.*

Fuck. I couldn't run away and hide like I wanted…not on the final day and not hours before the awards. The show must go on, despite the shitstorm…I mean, hell, Andrew and Marla? Blackmail and sex? My throat tightened and I had to clear my throat before responding. "Go ahead, Kay. What is it?"

"What's your twenty?"

"I'm on the far east lot where the overflow parking is. Need me over at the entrance tent?" *Please say no. Say no.*

"Nope. Someone was asking and needed to talk to you."

Someone. Rylan. *No, thanks.* "Ah, actually. I'm getting waved over on the south-east lot. I'll let you know when I'm done."

"There isn't a south—"

I clicked off my radio and gave myself ten minutes. Rylan wouldn't know I'd made up the location, but Kayla would and hopefully she understood my intention. I deserved ten minutes to mourn the promise of a relationship I'd been excited about…even looking forward to taking it further. That wasn't something I did lightly or often. I groaned, hitting my forehead with my fist, and took another long swig of whiskey. "Shit."

And to hear about Andrew fucking Marla? *Good god.* I rubbed my temples, replaying the words I'd overheard again and again. Him and Christine were going to run me out of a well-earned job to prevent...what? Marla's husband from finding out about one of her affairs? So Christine could keep her job? What hold did Christine have over Andrew and why did my eight years of hard work not matter to any of them?

Because people suck. They're selfish. That wasn't new information, but it didn't take the dull sting away. If I had known...no, if Rylan had told me about this, I could've come up with a plan of attack. Instead, I'd run out of there like an idiot and if it came down to it, Andrew had more money and could fire my ass for sleeping with Rylan.

"Ugh!" I hit the steering wheel, annoyed at myself for having all these conflicting feelings. I didn't know who I was madder at—Rylan, Andrew, Christine or myself. Probably a combination of all four. Andrew and Christine made sense. They held my career in their selfish little hands. But Rylan... The ache came and went in my chest. He'd made me feel capable and confident. Like starting my own show could be possible. Had he meant it or was he trying to cover up his own guilt about lying to me?

Thirty seconds. I gave myself thirty more seconds of pity before taking one last swig. Rylan didn't matter anymore. I knew I could do it—own my own show and make it better than Cruising Silvas had ever been.

Hell, I had thought about it fleetingly the past couple years, but his insistence on how I would succeed at it— coming from him—meant more than he knew. It could've all been a lie, but I had never let a man define my worth and I sure as hell wasn't going to start now. *Nope.* Moneybags would just be a fun memory in the future and all my energy had to go into dealing with Andrew. It was *my* turn.

One more swig of whiskey, one quick pep-talk to myself and I turned the radio back on and waited to see if anyone was desperately calling for me. It remained quiet and I had a shit list of people to go through. While I wanted Rylan to be the first, Christine seemed more likely. I knew her schedule and she owed me a goddamn explanation. Then I'd visit Andrew. Rylan would come later, if I was up to it, but at this point, he could go on his merry fucking way. If we said goodbye, great, if not…I'd be just fine.

He chose not to tell me. He let me sleep by him, each night. God, how long did he know?

No. No more. It was stupid to be upset over a four-day fling. Childish, even. I needed to focus on the fact that a VP and a CEO were trying to push me out of the business using various inappropriate methods. *Blackmail and sex? Is this a reality show? Jesus.*

Christine was always a mess on rewards day, organizing the line-up and printing the correct awards. It was a lot of work, each car needing six awards printed out depending on what it had won, and it took a lot of time. But instead of pitying her, I hoped she messed up big-time.

She usually yelled and darted around the tab room — the place where her small team counted and tallied the judges' score cards until the last minute — and had a wild look to her. I should've waited to confront her after the show. Hell, I should've confronted her the first day things got weird between us. But I wasn't feeling polite. *Nope. Not at all.*

I weaved through the people and parked myself outside the tab room. An odd sense of calm fell over me, the calm before the storm. I smiled at the judges waving at me and gave a nod to Gary, who had dark circles under his eyes. He, too, was always a mess on the final day, but as soon as Caravan started, he'd be done and ready to party. And man, he could party.

Ten more steps until I entered the room and a familiar cologne tickled my nose, but I ignored the tingling on the back of my neck. I knew what it could mean, but I didn't stick around to find out if *he* was near. Rylan was next on my list. I pushed the door open and found Christine alone in the room, bent over a table with about fifty folders in a pattern. "Christine, we need to talk."

"Okay, Kim, just let me — " She froze and dropped the folder in her hand. "Fern?"

"Yup." I leaned against the door, preventing anyone from entering the room. All color left her face. "Your guilty posture about answers my question, but I'd like to know why. We've worked together for eight years. Eight years, Christine."

"I'm so sorry, Fern." She burst into tears, her shoulders shaking with each breath, but I felt nothing but contempt for her. "I just found out this week...I caught them. He was going to fire me...he threatened me. You don't understand."

"I don't understand? You knew about the affair and were going to let him fire me because of your daughter's actions? It didn't matter my blood, sweat and tears I've put into this show because let's not forget, this is a fucking business? A company. Not a high school with drama and pettiness. But you seemed to forget that. You seem flustered...did I get it all correct? Did I leave anything out?"

She took another ragged breath and grabbed a bunch of tissues. "I'm so sorry. I have a house to pay for, the lawyers from all of Marla's shit she pulls where gets herself in trouble. If I lost this job...I don't know what I'd do."

"Mm. Glad to see your priorities. Tell me, how old is Marla? In her thirties? You're putting your own career on the table because she likes to sleep around? Not a smart move, Christine. Not at all. I'm going to finish the show because I'm a goddamn professional, but when it's over, I hope to never see your face again. It's been nice knowing you."

She tried blabbering more excuses or reasons, but none of them would make me understand her actions. Who would willingly screw over a co-worker? *Someone desperate. Someone I shouldn't've trusted.* My hands shook when I left her in the room with her tears and self-pity, but energy roared in my gut. They had walked over me for far too long and it was time to do what I'd squashed flat for all these years. *I won't repeat my mom's mistakes — I have a plan and a team with me.*

I was done with their bullshit and their manipulations. Rylan had been right about one thing — blaming all revenue on me was unacceptable when Christine's job brought in over half of our profit. *One down.*

My parents used to tell me it freaked them out how I could compartmentalize my life to the point of being a robot. Like the time we got in a car accident and the paramedic couldn't find my pulse. Or when we had a house fire and everyone cried, but I rescued our dog, called the cops and walked over to our neighbors to ask for a place to wait. This was like that...putting my varying emotions into different boxes until I could cope with them. Christine had hurt me, but it paled in comparison to knowing the company I had put my heart and soul into could throw me away for a hot piece of ass.

Fuck. A bubble of emotion crept into my throat and I fought the urge to cry. Andrew stood on the other side of the judging field, his sunglasses covering his eyes that I knew were following my every move. Was he thinking about firing me...causing a scene since he knew about me and Rylan? No. I couldn't see him yet. I needed to have all my ducks in a row before confronting him. I wasn't ready.

"Fern."

I tensed at Rylan's voice. I hadn't heard him sneak up toward my cart and I tried to think of a response. Anything to get him to go away. But he didn't pick up on my signals. He made the right choice to stay three feet away from me, but his soft and kind voice almost broke the barrier I had put up between us. "Are you doing okay? Kayla wouldn't tell me where you went and I haven't been able to think of anything else."

I gripped the wheel, counting to ten before meeting his gaze. Yeah, he looked worried and guilty as hell. But damn it, he'd played me...feeding me lines and lying, preventing me from coming up with a plan to get Andrew back. I smoothed down my shirt and focused on his black shoes instead. "I'm managing."

"We missed our chat at ten."

"Yeah, sorry. I was busy," I snapped, rubbing my temples and taking a long breath. "I've had some things I need to do since the startling news I learned just a couple hours ago."

"We need to talk about everything you heard or think you know." He lowered his voice and moved closer to me. My entire body tensed, craving his touch. My hormones were not on the same page as my heart and the battle inside my body was less than fun. "You can give me five minutes. Please, Fern."

"Fine. Get in."

His ass was an inch away from the seat before I pressed on the gas pedal. He gripped the bar and it brought me a little bit of joy when he let out a couple of cuss words. I had no location in mind. Nowhere was far enough from this place or pleasant enough for my thoughts and headspace, but if I'd learned anything about Rylan, it was that he was persistent. It would be easier to get it over with before talking to Andrew. *Ugh. The rat bastard.*

We drove past the entrance tent, past the first overflow parking lot and onto a back track that very few people knew about. He was smart enough to not talk or ask a single question the entire ride and I pulled up to a little shack. The venue was right next to a golf course and this was the ninth hole — also a beer hideout, I'd found out three years ago. I stopped the cart and chose the lone picnic table to sit down at. It was easier to face him rather than feel his heat next to me.

I pointed at the bench across from me. "Sit. Talk."

He lowered himself onto the seat, his gaze searching my face. I ignored the longing in his eyes, the way he swallowed real loud and the way the stress lines on his forehead hadn't left since we got here. It was torture, knowing how close I was to letting this become...something. But it was stupid to be this hurt after four days. It was too soon to be this upset.

"What's going on in your head, Fern? I need to know where you're at before I start."

He reached out a hand, only to pull it back at the last second. The sweet gesture about broke me because I wanted his comfort. I wanted his heat and strength, but too much had been done. My focus was on my job and my future. That was it.

"When did you find out about Andrew and Marla?" I clenched my legs together under the table, waiting on pins and needles to hear his answer. It mattered. It mattered so fucking much. His wince wasn't hopeful. He blanched and reached out for my hand again, but I shook my head. "No. Answer me."

"Tuesday night. They were going at it in the side building where they let me work."

Adrenaline rushed through my body, right before a heaviness took over my chest. My eyes stung and I tried blinking away the tears, but one escaped and he sucked in a breath. "Fern, please. It's not—I'm so sorry."

"Why didn't you tell me then? That was *two* nights ago."

He ran his hand over his jaw. A light beard had been growing the entire week and it somehow made him look better as it went on. His eyes were cloudy, regret evident, but I locked that info up and put it away. "The day before, you made it clear you didn't want to talk about business."

"Great, blame me," I fired back. He gave me a pointed stare and I fought the urge to flip him off. I prided myself on being mature but god, he brought out a crazy side of me.

"I'm outlining my thoughts, hoping you understand. The last thing I want to do is hurt you. I hope you realize this." His gaze heated over, our attraction still as strong as that first day, but I ignored it. "I don't know when it happened, I think maybe seeing you with vendors, how you handled them like a boss, but at some point, this started to get real between us. You know, beyond sex. It got complicated then because I wanted to tell you, but I was selfish. I wanted all the good parts and you've known me three days. You've worked with Andrew eight years and I panicked. It deserved to come from him."

"You could've told me and we could've...come up with a plan or something. I don't get it, Rylan."

He ran a hand over his face, exhaustion showing in his dark eyes. "You came to me the next night wanting to talk about business. It was perfect for two reasons. For starters, you deserve to run this show. That is evident as hell. My intentions of saying that to you had nothing to do with what I knew about him. Nothing. I swear to you. You have what it takes and I know you know that. If today is the last day I see you, please don't let that dream die."

I rubbed my forehead, digesting his words. It was the right thing to say, but he had always said the right thing. The entire week, he'd spewed lines and words that went straight to my soul. I groaned and jumped when my radio crackled. Kayla spoke again, her well-timed call giving me the space I needed. It got too intense.

"Big Cheese, we got some hot and bothered vendors wanting their deposit checks. Three of them started following me around and I had to call security to get them off me so I could go to the bathroom."

I snorted, avoiding Rylan's heavy stare and eyed my watch. "The show awards ceremony starts in an hour, I'll be there as soon as it ends. Tell them I have the checks and if they can find me, they'll get them."

"Ohhh, I like the sound of that. I take it you're enjoying the grass, huh?" She knew of our hideout and every year the two of us snuck out here for a beer or two.

"You got it, Little Cheese."

Shit. I used Rylan's nickname and for a split second, we had a momentary truce, both of us sharing a smile, as Kayla's cackle carried over. "See you soon."

I turned it down and gave Rylan a look stare. "We should get you back. You need to get your car lined up."

"We're not done talking."

"What is there to say? Your confidence in me starting a company was fueled by you knowing Andrew's secret. Our plans, our...*god*. I can't wrap my brain around it. It...it was fun while it lasted, but the lie is just too much for me."

"It wasn't a lie, Fern. My feelings for you are true. Hell, I know that. Before you heard what you did, my goal was to confront him and demand he tell you. He doesn't have a place in what we had—no, what we have. Because it's real and we both feel it. Can you admit that?"

He stared at me, his eyebrows furrowed together with the little dimple between them. Worry etched his face, but I forced myself not to think about it. I had to end what we'd started. It was safer that way. Hell, I felt betrayed after four days. What would happen if we let it continue a whole month? "Look—"

"I want more with you. I want to be with you. I looked at flights to St. Louis next weekend so I could see you again. I almost bought one, but I wanted to make sure we were on the same page. This is real for me, all of it." His eyes warmed and he reached out to squeeze my wrist for just a second. "I understand you're hurt, but my intentions were never to hurt or deceive you. I'm an honest guy, always have been. Keeping information from you might not have been my smartest move, but I'm hoping you can forgive me."

I shook my head. My emotions tumbled out and I couldn't focus on just one. Fifty-three minutes until the show started, potentially fifty-three minutes until I got to see Rylan for the final time. "We should head back."

He groaned, pinching the bridge of his nose, but got up and walked to the golf cart. He kept his distance for the ten-minute ride and gave me one long glance when I stopped the cart right by the orange cones signaling the judging zone. "I've enjoyed our time together, and I'm confident enough to say you did too. I'd be furious in your situation and while I'm selfish and want to demand we talk it out, I'll give you space. If you need anything…please find me."

He reached out, lightly trailing his fingers down my arms, and gave my hand one final squeeze before walking toward his Silvas. He was a fucking puzzle. Wanting to talk, giving me space, saying he wanted more…which I had too, until he'd lied.

Did he lie? my brain challenged me.

Yeah. He'd withheld information. Played me. Told me what I wanted to hear to deal with the guilt. *No.* He'd been upfront and explained his rationale and while I didn't like it, I knew in my gut he was telling the truth. He wasn't malicious. He wasn't cruel. But he was dangerous and my decision to push him away had been the right one. Of that, I was sure.

"Gah!" I hit the wheel for the tenth time that morning when two familiar figures approached me from the south.

"I'll be damned, Karl. Fernie's gone and finally lost her mind. Talking to herself and staring off into the distance. I knew this day would come, I tell you." Rich put his hand on my shoulder, Karl on the other side, and an odd calm came over me. They were my family. My rocks. A yearning to stay with them, with the company and the people, hit me hard. I couldn't say goodbye to this world. I loved it. The vendors, the stress, the weather and the hooligans. By god, Andrew wasn't going to take that away from me. *No fucking way.*

"You okay, girlie? Karl might be old, but he can kick some ass if you need him too."

I snorted and leaned into Rich for a second, his tobacco smell the same as it had been all these years. "I don't know. Maybe. Say, if I started my own Silvas show, would you two join me?"

"What kind of question is that, you silly girl?" Karl gave me an awkward noogie. "Rich and I have been arguing who should tell you to do just that. Of course, we'll follow you. I'd bet a pretty penny every single one of us clowns in the yellow shirts would follow you."

Those words caused me to finally break down. All the emotions, the compartmentalizing, the stress of the show, Andrew, Christine, Marla and *Rylan*. I'd survived all that, but two of my favorite old men telling me they'd follow me? That was my undoing. Rich handed me a handkerchief and Karl handed me a beer straight from his pocket. "Drink this, Fernie. It'll help with the mess you got on your face."

I laughed, sniffed and chugged the shitty pale beer. "Thanks, you guys. I needed that."

"It's what we do here, Fernie. We're family," Rich said, giving me another hug. In that gesture, I reset my to-do list.

Forty-five minutes until the awards ceremony. That was plenty of time to call the head of security, a lawyer… I needed Kayla here soon, too.

Then I'd have the final showdown with Andrew and burn his career to the ground. A plan was forming, one that was lethal…one that would give Andrew no choice but to hand over the company to me. It was brilliant and I wiped the tears from my eyes and clasped my hands. "Say, how do you gentlemen feel about a sneak attack? Want to help me save the company?"

Chapter Sixteen

Rylan

The sun beat onto my neck, the Midwest humidity clogging my throat, and it didn't matter how much water I drank. My thirst never went away and I chugged my second bottle in five minutes. Life was weird. It always kept going. Bad things happened all the time and the sun kept shining, and life went on. Like the passing of my dad. Like my mom losing a part of herself. Like the shit Fern's boss had pulled. And the end of something I really wanted.

It sucked and the dull ache in my chest hadn't left since she'd walked into the office. *Fucking bad timing.* I pulled my shirt from my skin, hoping to get some air flow in there, but it didn't help. The procession would start in ten minutes and everyone was on edge. The owners were pacing around their cars, biting their nails or scrambling to polish the hoods of their vehicles. It wouldn't make a difference — Christine had explained the judging process and how, after they'd done their initial inspection, nothing would change. Not bird shit, a dent, a scratch, or how shiny it was.

I sent a couple of texts to my family, a weighted sadness sitting on my shoulders as the week came to an end. The thought of losing myself in my business sounded inviting, diving into a new program and shutting down all thoughts of everything. Yeah. I would get the hell out of this city the second I got my car loaded.

Someone said my name, pulling me from my pitying thoughts. "Rylan. Get your ass over here."

Larry waved me over with a grin, and I walked toward his car. He handed me a lit cigar without asking. "Tradition."

The earthy sweet taste spread through my mouth, releasing through my nose in a big puff of smoke. I could count on one hand the amount of times I'd had a cigar, but I couldn't think of a better or more needed time. "Thanks."

"You look rough." He frowned and the lines on his weathered face came together in an odd pattern. If he thought I looked rough, then hell, I needed to pull myself together more.

"Women issues."

"Shit, that doesn't change. Married or not, women are a goddamn mystery. Beautiful but a pain in my ass. I never know what they're thinking and I've been with my fair share of ladies."

"I'm sure you have, Larry." We shared a brief smile, but the uncomfortable ball of emotion formed again. He stared at me for a long time, his old eyes searching for something. It didn't bother me. I was thankful to not sit alone with my thoughts and he finally nodded. "What?"

"Can't believe your old man's gone. He came to these shows for years but never brought the beaut. Good stock. Kinda thought he was full of shit talking about a '67 with cherry-red curves. Feel bad I didn't believe him." He took another puff, hacked into his fist and jutted his chin toward me. "How's your mom doing?"

"He talked about her?" Why that surprised me, I wasn't sure.

"Talked about all of you. Let me think...yeah. He talked about your sister, right? You got one. He talked about a son...You. Grandkids. He prided himself on his family and his car. I gave him hell for never bringing her, but he preferred being a spectator rather than an owner. I think he wanted to save money. Frugal. Planned to buy a camper and drive around the Midwest with your mom. Last we talked, he had a road trip mapped out for a month. Real excited about it. I told him to make sure he knew how to change a tire, cause if one of those babies popped in the mountains, he'd be screwed."

Fuck. I had no idea. The smoke burned my eyes and my breath caught in my throat—Larry knew more about my dad over the last couple of years than I did. Emotion clogged my voice and I used the excuse of the cigar to buy me extra seconds. When I felt ready to speak, I said, "I'm glad he came here all these years. This is a unique event."

"It's history. Years of families, owners, you name it. We support each other."

I took another puff of the cigar, fighting back emotion, when someone whistled. Christine stood at the head of the owner's lot with a megaphone and, at first glance, she looked rough. Red-rimmed eyes, her hair a mess and she blinked a lot. Part of me was happy she looked awful.

"Attention, owners, we are getting into position. Please line up as we planned and stop when you get to the X. We'll get your photo and it'll be shipped to you. If there are any spelling errors on your certificates, please wait until Thursday before calling our office. We aren't even looking at a phone for the next four days."

I patted Larry on the shoulder and put out the cigar before heading to Rayme. This was where we all sat in our cars and waited to see if our money had gotten us the certificate. I laughed when I started the car. Five days ago, I hadn't given a single shit about this place. The car was too extravagant, the people odd with their obsession with them, but now? Now it meant so much more. I'd met Fern. Larry. Damn it, I wanted the certificates for my dad. The man I hadn't made time to know.

It goes both ways. The lump in the back of my throat grew and I cleared it, wishing I had my bottle of water. I wished I could talk to Fern about it. She'd know the right thing to say, but the stab of regret hit me there, too. *God.*

"Let's move, people."

I whipped my gaze toward the voice and Fern stood at the head of the line, a camera on a strap around her neck. The two older gentlemen I saw her with a lot sat on chairs near her, narrowing their eyes at me. *Shit.* That couldn't be a good sign. I gave them a quick nod and continued watching Fern, how she held herself together even though her world had fallen apart mere hours ago. She stood tall, not giving Christine or Andrew any of her attention as she worked her ass off.

I didn't miss the fact that Marla — the photographer — was nowhere in sight.

Fern snapped pictures of the ten cars ahead of me, each owner saying some dumbass flirty remark...not that I could blame them. She looked amazing with her twisted bun, her long tan legs and the awful polo that she somehow made look good. Her smile was forced and her eyes were a little darker than normal, but she still stole my breath away.

When it was my turn, the only sign she knew it was me was a quick intake of breath. "Fern. Why are you taking pictures?"

"Because Marla disappeared. Move to the X, please." She pointed toward the pavement and refused to meet my eyes. It hurt. It fucking hurt, but I moved three inches farther and gave a tight smile for her to take the picture. She nodded and met my gaze for a second. It was then I saw her anguish. Her blue eyes were dull, a little red underneath them, and I would've done anything to put the light back into them. To fix it. To hold her and help her forget everything for an hour or so.

"Come by my room tonight. *Please*. I need to see you one more time," I begged. I never begged or pleaded or asked twice for a chance to talk to a woman. To be honest, I hated it.

Her breathing hitched, a slight twitch in her left eye, but that was all I received. Christine announced my name and I had to drive forward onto the circular driveway where everyone lined up.

"Rylan Cirula and his '67 have been awarded both Gold and Original Accreditation. These are the two highest awards one can get, signifying his Silvas is in pristine condition, the same as when it left the lot all those years ago. Congratulations, Mr. Cirula!"

Fern took more picture. Andrew stood there holding the awards and a grim expression on his face. He held out his hand and turned toward Fern with a fake-ass smile. It was disgusting and surreal — all the people who had disrupted Fern's life in the same area. She took the picture with a blank expression, the thin older man walking up to her and giving her shoulder a squeeze. She leaned in to him just a bit and walked toward the next car.

If that wasn't strength and loyalty, I didn't know what was.

"We're happy for you Mr. Cirula. Can't wait to see you next year," Christine said, clearly unaware I knew anything. Her gaze held no fear. But Andrew's...shit. His eyes spat fire at me, but what could he do? If he wanted to save face, he'd act mature. But it pissed me off that he clouded the moment my dad had craved.

His car had got the awards.

Fuck.

He got them too late. I clenched my jaw as I drove off the driveway and back toward the sandlot. I began loading my dad's car into the trailer. It was a long process, ensuring it rested correctly on the ramp. There couldn't be a single scratch or I'd hear about it, but I managed to load it without any issues, the lightweight feeling in my chest fluttering. *We won.*

I held the folder that had the two certificates in my hands and I called my mom. She answered on the first ring. "Hello, Rylan — how...how did you do?"

"We got the awards, Mom. Dad got finally got them."

She burst into tears, and I squeezed my eyes together at her blatant display of emotion. It was an odd combination—the guilt and the joy—but hearing my mother's sobs was the last wake-up call I needed. I had to make more of an effort for her. And I would. "Mom, did dad ever talk about a guy named Larry?"

"Larry? Yes. He did. Why?" She sniffed.

"Do you still want a camper? Do you want to take a week and travel? Once a year, we can go and visit any city you want. I'm sure Analisa and the kids would go. We could make it a family thing," I said the words, shocked that I did. I didn't volunteer to spend time with my mom. I never wanted to spend an entire week off work...but it was time I got over it. Life was too short.

"Oh, oh my. Rylan...this is...we can talk about this later." She sniffed a couple more times and cleared her throat. "Just enjoy the rest of the show and we'll get together when you get back. I'd like that, if you want?"

"I'd like it too, Mom." I smiled—the first time I had plans with one of my parents and I wasn't already dreading it. It was progress.

"Can you send me a picture of the awards?"

"Of course, Mom," I paused, unsure of what I wanted to say. "Look, I'm...sorry. I've never felt closer to Dad than being here and I've learned a lot about him this way. I can't let what happened with him and me happen to us. I'll be around more. I promise."

She let out another cry and Analisa's voice picked up. "This better be good news why Mom's crying like a hyena."

"We got the awards. I admitted I haven't been the best son...it was an emotional morning. I love you guys."

"Jesus fucking Christ," she replied and my mom scolded her for language, even through her tears. "Are you drunk?"

"No. Just a dumbass."

"I won't argue with you there. But thanks, Ryno. Love you too. I gotta go… Mom's trying to get into the wine again."

She hung up and I double-checked the trailer. It was all closed tight and I desperately tried to think of anything else I could do to stay. But there was nothing.

I had *nothing* holding me here anymore. I was free to head back to Chicago and stay in my own bed, get back to work on a business I loved like a firstborn. *But…* It was the but that kept me there, waiting for something. Hoping for someone to talk to me. *Larry!* I needed to see if he'd won any awards. That was it. I'd head back to the award show and see what Accreditation he got. I even chose to walk back — prolonging my time there — and my sunburned neck regretted it.

Larry had got Silver and Bronze Accreditation and I snuck three more glances at Fern before accepting defeat. I would go back to the hotel and check out early — my original plan had been to spend one final night with Fern before leaving in the morning, but why wait?

I took a deep breath, wishing like hell we'd exchanged numbers, when the buzzing of the golf cart stopped toward the back of the sandbox and, sure enough, Fern got out and walked right toward me. My heart soared. She was coming back. *Thank god.* I almost ran to her but managed to lean against the side of my SUV.

For a reconciliation that hopefully would end in bed, she looked sad. Too sad. In fact, her expression had my entire body tensing for bad news. It looked like a goddamn goodbye.

"Congrats, Ry. Your dad's car got both certs." She gave me a weak smile.

"Thank you."

She traced a line in the gravel with both feet before meeting my gaze. The same dull blue eyes were there, not the vibrant ones I'd gotten used to. "I bet you're feeling pretty good."

"It's a mixture. I called my mom, she sobbed. It'll be a good thing to bring us together."

"Good. That's good." She gulped and traced the line again. "I brought you something."

"Yeah?" A tiny bit of hope burst inside me, desperately latching on to whatever she wanted to give me. "What is it?"

She chewed on her bottom lip and pulled out a bag from her pocket. "It's nothing big. Just, the pins, pennants and ribbons from this year. I figured your nephews and mom might want them to help commemorate the win. You won and I know it's a big deal for your family."

I bit back another wave of emotion and moved to her. She didn't put up a fight when I wrapped my arms around her in a huge hug. I breathed in her sweet scent, enjoying the soft curves of the strong woman who'd snuck her way into my life. I kissed her neck, ignoring how tense she got. "Thank you. *Thank you.*"

"You're welcome." She slid down my body, giving me a slight shove. The distance between us grew and grew, the gap widening and my hope disappearing. "I also came to say goodbye."

Punch. To. The. Gut. "I'm going to need you to be real clear here. Is this a goodbye until later? A see you later?

Or goodbye as in I never get to see you again? Because I really hope it's not the third option, Fern."

She blinked a little too fast and gave me a grimace instead of a smile. "I wouldn't say never. If you're at another Silvas show sometime—"

"Stop." I hid my hurt and squeezed the bag containing all the pins. "Then I shouldn't expect to see you tonight?"

"N-no." She shook her head and gave me a watery smile. "This week was…fun. Thank you."

"You're thanking me? Fuck that." Anger replaced hurt and my patience had already run thin. "We're adults, so I'm not going to beg you, but I think I at least deserve a reason. Tell me. Why is this goodbye for you?"

"Because…because I need to deal with the fallout of all this." She waved her hand around in a circle and refused to meet my gaze. She chose to look at the ground instead of me, despite how intimate we had been. "And I can't afford any distraction. I'm sorry."

I nodded, a little too aggressively, and stepped away from her. "Goodbye then."

"Good luck, Ry." She finally looked me in the eye, her torment and indecision clear as day. But if she couldn't talk to me about it, then I wouldn't waste my time. I cupped her chin and pressed my lips against hers, hating it would be the last kiss I'd have with her. She melted into me, but I cut it off. She had made up her mind so I left her there, standing in the road looking all sorts of sad.

Feelings suck.

Chapter Seventeen

Fern

The black SUV left a trail of dust when Rylan sped off, leaving the grounds and me behind. I rarely made decisions I regretted because life was too short for regrets. They were all learning opportunities and it was how I dealt with a lot of strife. But this decision, though—it might be the first time I wished I hadn't done what I did. My reason for ending it wasn't false, but it was a cop-out.

Five days with him had turned me into a mess. I didn't do the whole *mess* thing. I was known as the calm one, the composed and mature one, and letting Rylan in for even five days had almost been too much. If I wanted to start a company on my own, I had to remain focused and without drama.

Andrew is the drama, not Rylan.

I shook my head and let myself mope for another two minutes. The Silvas Caravan was starting in ten minutes and Kayla began handing out the vendor checks. My favorite side-kick took one look at me and grabbed the envelopes from my hand. "Go talk to him. Now."

I did, but the unsettled feeling remained. But, as life had taught me, the show would go on. I wanted to drink whiskey and laugh with Karl and Rich, but I wouldn't allow myself that joy until I'd gotten through my final task. *Andrew.*

My blood boiled at the thought of his name. It didn't help that I'd gotten stuck taking pictures of him shaking hands with every owner. I cringed and fought the urge to throw up. I had never gone from being content with someone to hating them so aggressively that I couldn't think straight.

That was what Andrew's actions had done. Christine's too.

I took a couple of breaths and put my emotions back in their boxes, shoving the sadness and grief away until later. It was attack mode, driven by righteous anger now. Our plan had been set, the pieces were in order and I wanted to checkmate his ass. Switching gears from Rylan to Andrew, I got back into the golf cart and plastered on a fake smile the entire drive.

It went shorter than I would've liked because whatever happened in there, that was it.

I parked, smoothed down my shirt and about ran into Rich carrying two large beers. "Sorry, old man."

"I'll forgive you once," he replied with the positivity I needed. He darted his gaze to the offices and back to me. "Are you ready?"

"As ready as I can be. Everything good on your end?"

"Sure thing, Fernie." He lifted a beer in a salute and smiled.

I'd told him and Karl everything after my meltdown and while they weren't shocked, they were mad on my behalf and I had never been more thankful that I had them to lean on. They'd helped formulate the plan, but it would be me and me alone facing Andrew in there. "Kayla's uncle should be here by now. Remember, if I'm not out in thirty minutes, bring the brigade."

"Don't leave any evidence," he whispered and I snorted. "You got this, Fernie."

I *did* have this. The glass doors shone with the high sun reflecting off them, and the air shifted the second I walked in. Andrew sat at the center table, an unreadable look on his face. He was nursing a beer and had his feet propped up on another chair, and his only greeting was pointing to the chair across from him. For a man on the brink of disaster, he looked a little too relaxed and it pissed me off.

I didn't sit down, but I moved to stand behind the chair and held on to the backrest. He opened his mouth, but I held up a finger. This was my show. "I have a lot of things I want to say to you, Andrew, and none of them are good. I just can't fathom how you could do this to me. We've worked together almost a decade and this..." I gripped the back of the chair and gathered more strength. "This show wouldn't happen without me. Do you realize everything I do?"

He stared at me blankly and I slammed my hand on the table. "Answer me!"

"Y-yes. I know you work extremely hard."

"That's not what I asked. Do you know what I do? Say it out loud."

"Uh, vendor registration and operations." His face turned bright red and he kept rubbing his hands over the back of his neck. *Good.* He looked nervous now. *About damn time.*

"Wrong. I do the marketing, the signage, vendor layout, registration, check-in day, I collaborate with Gary on recruiting and inviting club members, get our sponsors, do photography, help design the merch to sell, work with security and I fucking kick ass at all of it. What do you do?"

Holy shit, I was on a roll and couldn't stop.

"Fern—I know how valuable you are to this company."

"You were fucking Christine's daughter and were going to fire me. You don't just do that to people if you value them. Not as a respectful CEO. You don't." I paced the room and took another long breath. "I want the company. Every piece of it."

"Excuse me?"

"I didn't stutter, Andrew. I want the company. I want you, Christine and Marla out."

"It doesn't work like that," he began but his eyes bugged out a little bit and let out a long cuss word. "Fucking shit."

"What?"

"You conspired with Rylan, didn't you?"

"Uh, no." *Conspired? What?* "Don't change the subject."

"He came in here, threatening to buy me out if I didn't tell you. Then he demanded I sell it to you or I'd regret it." He cradled his head in his hands for a couple of seconds before he shook his head. "You're going to start your own show."

"You aren't a total idiot, then. Yeah. I will if you don't resign and give me this one." I ignored his comment about Rylan even though my heart about burst through my chest. "Everyone will follow me. Vendors. Kayla. Rich, Karl, Gary. You damn well know they will. Why do you think I was at the judges' dinner last night? I'm taking judges, too. You put the burden of raising revenue on me for all these months... I lost so much sleep because of this. When I punch the numbers, I bet my ass the operations side made more money than any other year. But what about Christine? Authentication has been on the decline and you know it."

I snapped my fingers and continued, letting out every ill thought I had. "But, oops, you couldn't fire Christine because you were hoping Marla would be with you. Fun fact, bud, she picks a guy every year and tries to milk anything out of him. Last year it was your buddy Ken. The year before, your brother Allen."

His face paled even more and he clutched the side of the table. I didn't feel an ounce of pity for him. He'd let his dick ruin his career and while it was shitty, he deserved it.

"I take it you didn't know about Marla. That's too bad, though. That's the thing about her, she's discreet. Her husband never finds out about her affairs. This time...quite a few of us know. Where do you think she ran off to? Back home, hoping to prevent Mark from finding out about it."

"Are you—don't fucking lie to me," he roared this time.

"You aren't in a position to demand anything from me. But I'm not lying."

"She's...I love her." He looked so helpless and pathetic, which he was. I snapped my fingers and gave him a condescending nod.

"It makes sense now. Why you stopped including me on meetings, only telling me the loss of funds every time you saw me. You hid how poorly the other areas were going because if I knew, I would push back against you. You couldn't just fire me, though, too many questions. But if we lost revenue and you could pin it on me, then you'd have a clear conscience."

I laughed and shook my head with the decision right there. Blackmail wasn't the route I would've chosen, but Cruising Silvas was my home and I wanted it. "I'm going to give you three options."

He winced and mumbled, "Jesus, you sound like your rich boyfriend."

His comment fired me up in the best way. *Pride.* I took it and stood a little taller. "Good. Then you better listen. Option one. Resign, give me the company. Option two. Keep the company, but damn well know I'm going to steal every one of your patrons. No one is loyal to you, but they are to me. Kayla is already out there, telling them the location is going to change next year with new leadership. Rich and Karl already have a lead on a venue."

He gulped and sweat formed on his forehead. I leaned over, doing my best impression of looking scary, and lowered my voice. "Option three. I do what I want anyway and make sure Mark knows about everything. Because while your dick might make your decisions, my brain makes mine. Look up, Andrew. Security cameras. And guess who's on my list of loyal clients already vowing to come with me? Mac. Head of security here. Think it'll be difficult to get him to get me a copy of the video?"

That broke him. A man I'd worked for most of my life fell apart into sobs and I felt nothing. I might feel regret in a couple of days, but right now, I felt high on life.

"What option do you pick? I never stop working, unlike you and Marla, so my plans start tonight."

"I-I don't care. I've wanted to sell so many times the past couple years. I-I just can't believe Marla...it was different with her."

"No, it wasn't." I radioed to Kayla for the next part of the plan. "Little Cheese, please bring the requested materials."

"Got it, boss."

She entered the room, winking at me, and placed the contract on the table. Kayla not only had an uncle who was an attorney, but her aunt was a notary and lived in town. Her aunt followed her, along with her uncle, and Andrew's face turned a ghastly white. "What—what is this?"

"Sign the document, Andrew, making it official that the company now belongs to me. I own all the stocks, control payroll and have the right to fire any employee. You will no longer be allowed in our offices and cannot under any circumstances try to sue us." I pushed the paper at him and handed over the pen from my pocket.

His watery gaze darted from person to person before his shoulders sagged. He signed the form—all eight places—and I handed it to Kayla's uncle. "It's official. Cruising Silvas is mine."

"Fuck, yeah!" Kayla jumped up and down, throwing her arms around me and spinning around. "I'm so happy for you. My god."

"Let's get out of this office and tell our crew." I slung my arm around her and didn't give Andrew another glance. He was old news. Garbage. Not my issue anymore and good lord, I felt like I'd lost ten pounds. We walked outside and Rich, Karl and all the noodlers stood there, their faces frozen as they waited for news.

I held up my hands and cheered. "I expect you all to call me Big Cheese now."

Applause, cheers and cries of joy met me. After hugs, high-fives, a couple of noogies and one awkward kiss on the top of my head from Rich, I eyed my new crew. "Rich and Karl, I expect you two to head vendors at least two more years before you retire for the third time. Kayla, Little Cheese, would you please be my VP of operations? It would be full-time, not just a summer gig."

She cried, doing an awkward jig before agreeing with too much excitement.

It was the best moment of my life, but one person was missing. Kayla bumped her hip against me. "BC, your face just fell. You can't be getting regret this fast."

"No, no. It's not that."

"Man problems," Rich joined our conversation and Kayla gave me a long look. "That fancy rich guy really got to her."

"Moneybags is smoking hot, though."

"You know his nickname?" I gave her an odd look. She blushed, giving me a little shrug.

"I've read the article about him a couple of times and recognized him that first day. I was so embarrassed I stuttered. It's that smile. He looks so good."

"I told him it was over. We were done. But Andrew told me what he said and...I feel stupid for not believing him."

"Love makes people do dumb shit. That's my motto," Karl added and gave me another half hug. "Groveling works."

"It's been five days. It's stupid, right?" I scanned my friends' faces but not one of them thought I was crazy. They shrugged and Kayla pointed to her watch.

"Our after-party starts at the hotel in two hours. I think that gives you plenty of time to *grovel* and join us at the fire pit. Feel free to bring Moneybags."

"What if it's too late? We never exchanged phone numbers because it was part of the fun. What if he left already?" My voice broke a little as worry took over.

"Then I know how to break into Christine's system and steal his phone number."

"God, I love you, Kay." I snorted and waved goodbye to my team. "I gotta go find him and I'll see you all later?"

"Sounds good, Big Cheese!"

Kayla snapped a couple pictures and I took off toward my car, desperate to make it back to the hotel to see if he was there. He could've gone back to Chicago. Why wouldn't he? I told him we'd never see each other again. *Goddamn not having his number.*

Christine. She leaned against the garage where we all parked and my gut tightened. I had no idea what to say, but she started. "You earned this. All of it. Your first assignment shouldn't be firing me, so I'm resigning. I'm so ashamed I got caught up in Marla's affairs. I'm so sorry, Fern."

"Thank you. I accept your resignation and while I'm not a fan of you right now, give it time. You were a large part of my life...but I need space."

"You're too kind. Thank you."

I gave her a curt nod and started my car. I chose to opt out of playing music and digested the day's events as I drove. Rylan wanted more with me. I owned Cruising Silvas. I wanted more with him.

Jesus, my life's gotten exciting.

I giggled, more out of nerves than happiness, and sped down the road toward our hotel. There was no

SUV or trailer in the parking lot and my hopes sank. I parked terribly and jogged toward the elevator, my leg bouncing up and down the entire ride up to his floor. His room was third to the right and I knocked as hard as I could.

My body froze, desperate for a sound or a clue he was there. It remained silent. No padded footsteps, no sound at all. I sank to the floor, the momentary hope disappearing as fast as it had come. I would give myself ten minutes to wallow, then I was having Kayla break into the system and enjoying whiskey with my team.

Yeah—ten minutes. I owed it to myself.

Chapter Eighteen

Rylan

I was a fucking idiot. Plain and simple. I should've give her my number, gotten hers — something besides being as dramatic as hell and driving away. She remained in my rearview mirror, her posture nothing like the bold confident woman I'd fallen for. She stood there until I turned to leave the grounds and the vision burned behind my eyelids. She couldn't have meant the words. Her body had told me in every way possible she hadn't wanted to say them, but she had. I should've tried harder. I made a fist and thought about punching the bar top.

The first night we'd met was in the hotel bar, and a small part of me hoped she'd look here, or come here. Stress built around my shoulders, the shitty bottom of the shelf whiskey not taking any of my edge off. Not when I should be with her, congratulating her on the end of the show, celebrating my Accreditation s and planning our future together—any future we could figure out. The ache behind my forehead started, pain pounding with each beat of my heart. *Shit.*

"Another one, sir?" the same young bartender from the first night asked me with a cheery smile. "You look like you need one."

"No, thanks," I replied. My jaw hurt from grinding my teeth and working myself to sleep seemed like a better idea. Work had been my clutch for fifteen years—now was no different. While I wouldn't call it a heartbreak, it rivaled one. "Charge it to my room, please."

He gave a curt nod and there was no other distraction to avoid heading back up *alone.* My watch read seven—the after-party Fern had told me about started soon. Would she go? Had she quit? Was she happy? Had she confronted Andrew and busted his balls...*god, I hope she did.*

Resolving to call her, email her, or even just find out what happened, I went into the elevator, formulating my next move. She wasn't leaving the hotel until tomorrow. *A note.* I'd leave a note on her door with my contact information and it'd be left up to her. Her confidence and take-no-shit-from-anyone attitude had entranced me the first night...and when she'd flipped my line on me, offering to take me to my room, she'd caught my interest. *Yup.* I'd leave a note. Possibly camp outside her hotel room, but that might cross the line. *Flowers and a note are better.* Confident in my decision, I nodded to myself just as the elevator doors pinged. I took one step and froze.

Fern sat against my door, her eyes closed, hair up in her crazy bun, and my heart leapt to my throat. I ran to her, stopping just before touching her. "Fern! Are you okay?"

She opened her eyes — the clear blue returning — and it was as if a fist squeezed my heart. Her lips stretched into an odd-looking grin, her jaw becoming a little slack. "You're still here."

"Yeah." I kneeled, running my hands over her arms, seconds away from pulling her into me. Something was off and concern took over. "Are you okay?"

"Yes. More than okay. Well, the jury is still out." Her gaze never left my face and she gave me an expression I hadn't seen on her before — and I wanted to understand it.

Her words didn't make any sense to me and I carefully intertwined our fingers. She glanced at our hands, a sad smile now on her face, and I pressed a quick kiss to the back of her hand. "What are you doing outside my door?"

"I wanted to see you."

"Yeah?" I bit back a grin and my breath caught in my throat. Hope blossomed again, but this time, there wasn't a ball of dread in my stomach. It felt right. "Why's that?"

She got onto her knees and put her hands on my shoulders. While she touched me, it wasn't nearly enough. I yanked her against me, crushing her against me. Her sweet floral perfume clogged my nose in the best fucking way and all the tension left. We'd be alright.

"I needed to talk to you," she mumbled into my neck, her arms squeezing tight against me. "I thought you left."

"I planned on it," I said. I rubbed her, holding the nape of her neck in my hand.

"I'm so glad you didn't," she said. Her voice shook a little and when I tried to pry her away from me, she held on tighter. "I might've interrupted you from something. Can I, uh, can I come in?"

I chuckled and picked her up. She still clung to me, her lush body pressed against mine, and every emotion I had went haywire. "You're holding on to me real tight. I don't have a choice, do I?"

"Shit, I'm sorry." She immediately let go, embarrassment flooding her face. The reddening made her eyes stand out and I cupped her chin. She blinked a couple of times and her nervousness was cute as shit. I kissed her. It wasn't a goddamn goodbye kiss this time. It was a promise, a conversation. It was desperate and relieving when she opened her mouth, moaning the sounds that drove me crazy. But she stopped it too soon. She leaned her forehead against my mouth, her breathing a little ragged. "Ry, I'm sorry for my reaction."

"I'm sorry for how everything played out. I take it things went well?"

"You're the first person I wanted to call, but I didn't have your number so I ran here and was going to beg you to forgive me and let us try again. You weren't here…fuck. I can't get my thoughts straight."

"Glad my body flusters you."

"It's not just that. I mean yes, you're…we're…look, Rylan." Her voice changed. It became stronger and the fire grew in her eyes. But it was the good kind of fire. Not the kind I'd seen earlier where her words had torn me apart. "It didn't make sense in my mind to develop any sort of feelings for you after knowing you five days. It didn't make sense for me to be so upset when I thought you'd kept something from me. But life doesn't make sense, does it?"

"No, it doesn't."

She smiled at me, pushing her loose hair behind her ears and chewing on her bottom lip. I'd seen every part of her body but this, her confession in the middle of a hotel in my least favorite city in the world... This was the fucking best. "You came at the most chaotic part of my life, but I want you to stay. I want more with you. I don't know what that means, but I want it. If you're still willing to try, with me —"

She broke off when I attacked her mouth.

I had to have her.

All of her.

She gasped when I picked her up and slammed her back against the hotel door — so similar and so different from the night I'd met her. She moaned when I sucked her tongue. I needed more of her. A kiss wasn't enough. "Ry — we're in the hallway."

"Don't care," I said between kissing her. I fumbled with the hotel key with one hand and held on to her with the other. Our teeth clashed together and as soon as the door opened, I pressed her against the wall. Her hands were everywhere, tearing at my shirt and belt. I unbuttoned her shorts and she wiggled out of them, all while not breaking our mouths apart.

It was a goddamn feat.

"Naked. I need you naked," she panted when I set her on the ground. She whipped off her shirt and bra in two seconds, standing there completely bare for me. "Ry, please."

"Hold on, babe."

Her gaze heated over at the pet name, but I barely registered it. Her body... Sweat glistened between her magnificent breasts, her trim hips forming the perfect hourglass figure. I ran my hands from her neck to her legs, her pink nipples hardening and her breathing catching. My pulse raced, but I wanted to enjoy her. *Look at every inch of her. Cherish her.* "You're so fucking beautiful."

I brought my lips right above her heart, then moved along her chest until I got to her neck. She let out the tiniest groan and I gripped her waist. I licked a line from right beneath her ear to her taut nipples, sucking one point into my mouth as hard as I could. She arched her back and fisted my hair in her hands — it felt magical.

"I love this," she moaned.

"Mm." I trailed kisses and bites to her other breast, taking my time teasing her. I blew on the peak, goosebumps breaking out all over her body. "Beautiful. Can't get enough."

She trembled and her head fell back, hitting the wall. "Shit."

"I was being selfish. Come on, I want to spend hours cherishing you in bed." I picked her up and carefully set her on the made bed. Her blue eyes were the color of the sky right before sunset and an odd calm came over me. She was the right decision. But then she frowned. "Why the face, Fern? I thought you liked it when I did this."

I spread her thighs wide open and licked from her clit to her mouth. She bucked and let out a cry — but then pushed me over so she was on top. "Woah."

"I love it when you have your tongue on me. Hell, your fingers, months, dick... I love all of it all over me," she replied in a ridiculously sexy and husky voice.

I reached behind her and pulled out the ponytail, making her hair fall down around her. It was the sexiest thing I had ever seen. "I want it all with you."

Her face warmed, her fingers clawing at my chest until she brought her mouth to mine. She smiled, kissing me through the grin. "Ditto, handsome."

That about did it. I flipped her over again, reaching into my pants pocket to grab a condom. But when I sat on the edge of the bed to put it on, she moved to wrap her legs around me and reached around to fist my shaft. I hissed, the hot sensation bursting from my spine to my cock. "Wh-what are you doing?"

"You're not the only one who gets to enjoy foreplay, Ry."

She pumped me with her right hand, trailing her other hand up my inner thigh, and I bucked a couple of times. "Your cock is so smooth. I'm glad I get more time with him."

I gave a restrained laugh and removed her hand from me. "I want to orgasm with you, babe, not like this."

"That can be arranged."

She laughed when I attacked her. The condom was on and right before I slipped into her, we froze. Time stopped for those five seconds, where our gazes met and everything seemed okay. *Us. Our future.* Words I had never said almost spilled out, but I held them back. Fern seemed to understand and brought her hand to my face, giving me a little nod. *I know. Me too.*

Then I lost myself inside her, the pleasure of her body my own version of heaven. She met me thrust for thrust, both of us finding the perfect rhythm to bring us as much pleasure as possible. Her stomach tightened and I arched her hips up so her clit got the right pressure, and she exploded around my cock, her grip slipping from me with the sweat. *"Ry, yes!"*

It did me in. My restraint snapped and the burn started at the base of my spine, spreading through every limb I had as an orgasm so strong took over, causing stars to burst behind my eyes. "Fucking hell. Fern. Wow."

"Yeah. Same." She panted, pushing her hair out of her face as I pinned her down. I wasn't done with her. Not by a long shot. "Ry...you just came and you're giving me the bedroom eyes."

"It's you." I pulled out of her and quickly removed the condom, tossing it into the trashcan a foot away from the bed. I rolled onto my side and kept my hand on her hip, not able to fully leave her alone. "Please tell me we can stay in here all night, naked and together."

She rolled her eyes and scooted close enough that our noses almost touched. "I have the after-party and...well...since I'm the new boss, I should be there."

"Wait—what?" I froze. "What did you say?"

"I own Cruising Silvas now."

"Fern. *Fern.*"

The biggest smile I had ever seen crossed her face, almost making her look a little scary. "I know. I confessed everything to Rich—who convinced me to tell Kayla and Karl. We came up with a plan with Kayla's quick thinking. Her uncle's a lawyer and he served as the witness." She scrunched her nose and spoke fast, her excitement spilling out of her. "I was a boss, Ry. I laid it on the line for him, giving him three options, all of which ended up either with me starting my own company and taking all his employees, or him resigning and giving me control. He took the second route."

"Fuck. Holy shit. I'm so proud of you." I yanked her against me and hugged her. I had never felt such pride for another human being before — it was weird. My ears rang, my chest hurting with the rapid beating of my heart, and I was torn between wanting to scream with joy or ravishing her all over again. "I knew it. I knew you could do it."

She giggled in my ear and put her hand right above my heart, pushing me back. "Look, I'm not worried about what's in store for us anymore, but I do need to explain some things."

"Yeah?" I tensed a little, still raw from our almost-breakup hours ago. Five days wasn't enough to have a solid foundation of trust, but we would get there. I knew we would. "What is it?"

"You had no reason to try and play me. I assumed it because it was easier to blame everyone for what Andrew did to me. He told me what you did, what you said. And while I'd like to think I would've come to you eventually...his words confirmed what I knew. I have no reason not to trust you and while it takes me quite a bit of time to let people into my life, you snuck on it instantly."

"Ditto."

"I have one more apology."

"Did you actually say sorry?" I teased and she stuck her tongue out at me. I held up my hands. "Sorry, carry on, woman."

"Your confidence in me running a company shattered for about two hours. That was my fault. I know what my strengths are and the drama of everything made me forget. I've busted my ass and can handle running the show and I needed to realize that on my own. My hang-up from my mom's failure had too much impact and I blamed you as a scapegoat. I'm sorry. There. That's my final apology."

"For future reference, apologies should only be done naked and like this. You're easy to forgive when you're this fucking cute."

She gave me a sheepish grin. I used the break to push hair behind her ear. "For the record though, Fern, I would've bought the company and sold it to you — with or without being in a relationship. That wasn't a lie or a trick to tell Andrew. You're worth the investment."

She blushed and brought her lips to mine, taking her time kissing me. It was slower, sensual with long lashes of our tongues and hums of approval. "We're really doing this thing, huh?"

"I'm buying a ticket to see you next weekend as soon as I get up from bed. Can I stay with you or should we stick to hotels for a while?" I kissed her shoulder and enjoyed the way she molded her body against me, fitting just like a puzzle piece.

"You can stay with me. But I was thinking...after cleanup tomorrow, I don't have to be in the office for two weeks." She raised her eyebrows at me and in a weak voice, she asked, "Could I maybe come visit you in Chicago? I've been there twice and it's my vacation. If you're busy, it's not a big deal."

"You silly, naïve, beautiful woman." I rolled on top of her and kissed the tip of her nose. It was cheesy as fuck, but I didn't care. I wanted her, the relationship, the whole thing. "From here on out, you can come visit me any time. Any day. No questions. When I'm all in to something, I mean it. I'm all in. And until something changes, it'll remain that way."

"Yeah?" Her lip trembled a bit and I kissed it. "That's intense."

"It's the only way to live. I know what I want. Do you want help tomorrow and you can drive back with me?"

"It's not too soon?"

"Fern. I've licked every part of you. You know more about me than people I've known for years. It is not too soon. But it's up to you. There's no pressure here, okay?"

She sighed and moved to set her feet on the ground. She blinked a couple of times and ran her fingers over the top of the bed. She remained that way, silent, for a minute or two before she gave me that smile. "We need to get dressed. And look nice."

"Why?"

"Might as well get this over with. You need to come officially meet everyone."

Is she for real? "As?"

"I feel fourteen, but boyfriend? Partner? Lover? The term doesn't bother me but I'm all in, too." She winked and quickly put on her clothes. "Meet me upstairs in ten minutes."

She didn't wait before leaving the room and I scrambled to throw on a nice pair of slacks and a button-down. I sprayed an extra squirt of cologne and grabbed my wallet, keys and phone. It buzzed in my hand.

Unknown: Put me in your phone as Sexy Big Cheese.

I grinned hard and took off toward her room. She'd left the door open for me and I stormed in to find her leaning over the bathroom sink, applying a clear coat of lip gloss. "How'd you get my number, Fern?"

"I asked my new VP to break into the system for your number. I'm a boss-ass bitch now."

"You're going to be the end of me. You know that, right?" I slid behind her and wrapped my arms around her waist. "I'm totally okay with it."

She grinned at me in the mirror and her expression had so many promises. "I accept that position. Now, let's go meet my work family. They won't know what to do with themselves."

"Why's that?"

"You're the first guy I've brought, metaphorically, home."

"Aiming to be the last, too."

She leaned into me, a light sound of content escaping her. "You and your words. Let's go, handsome. Prepare yourself."

"I can handle anything, Sexy Big Cheese." I swatted her ass and followed her out of the hotel room, content and excited for whatever the hell life wanted to throw at me next. She took my hand and life was good.

Epilogue

Five months later
Fern

The cool almost-winter air blasted us both, our cheeks wind-burned despite the wool scarves we had wrapped around our faces It was uncharacteristically cold for November in St. Louis, but I wasn't ready to begin hibernation. I forced Rylan to take a walk around my favorite park. It was a twenty-minute drive from my two-bedroom loft and he hadn't complained once. In fact, he had been more quiet than normal since he'd gotten into town the night before. Typically, we got naked for the first two hours, then we had coffee, staying up all night talking and acting like teenagers. I squeezed his hand through our gloves and forced him to look at me. "Ry, we can head back if the cold is getting to you."

He rolled his eyes and removed the scarf covering his mouth. "I live in the Windy City, babe. This is nothing."

"Then what's going on? Normally, you talk my face off and I have to shut your ass up by taking off my clothes. I haven't had to resort to it yet today. I'm a little concerned."

His hazel eyes warmed for a second and he dropped a kiss on my mouth before letting out a long sigh. "I'm okay...been thinking a lot about the future."

"What about it?"

He gave me a thoughtful look and for the first time in any relationship I'd had, I didn't have the prickle of fear or worst-case scenarios going through my head. I had no doubt how he felt about me, about us, and instead of questioning his lack of explanation, I nudged his hip with mine. "Let's keep walking. When you're ready to talk about it, let me know. And if not, I'm perfectly content just being with you. Just think of what we can do to warm up when we get back to my place. I'm thinking...hot cocoa, sans-clothes and an action movie."

He gave me a slow, panty-melting grin, and continued walking with me. We passed a couple of benches, trees that had turned brown and barely hung on to their leaves, and an occasional jogger. I loved fall, the colors and smells. But after visiting Chicago, I had to admit it was prettier up there. It was dull here with gray skies and weak trees.

The future. What a frightening concept for most. He cleared his throat but didn't stop moving forward. I tried to remove my hand from his grip to adjust my scarf, but he held on tighter. I fought a giggle. He didn't realize how much he always touched me. It didn't matter where we were —, he hated distance between us. It was endearing and I'd grown to relish it. "Did Kayla find a new set of offices for you?"

Okay, we're talking about the show now. I kept pace. "She put an offer on it but isn't sure when she'll hear back. It was a bit outside our price range, but they were amazing. It was a loft with exposed brick and the views are to die for."

"Hmm. I hope you get it."

"Thanks?" My pulse raced a little bit more, curiosity not concern taking over. The silence grew a little more and I tried not to let it affect me. "Did I tell you Christine wrote me a letter?"

"Did she? What about?"

"Apologizing. Asking for forgiveness. Volunteering to help train whoever we hire for her position. I'm really thinking about splitting it with Kayla. It'll be a lot of work, but at least I'd know it would be done right."

He scowled and released my hand, stopping us right by a lake. Worry lines were etched on his forehead, but it didn't make him any less handsome than all those months ago when I'd met him. He was amazing and warmth spread through my veins. Our relationship worked for us. The past five months had been split between here and Chicago and a million phone calls in between. "I think you should hire someone for it. You don't want to spread yourself too thin. You've been working more than normal lately and well...yeah. You deserve some time off."

I rolled my eyes and pulled down on the lapel of his jacket. He gave me the leverage I needed and I pressed my cold lips against his. He melted into me, the little grumpiness he'd carried disappearing when I looked into his eyes. "Are you going to share why you seem to have a tiny stick in your ass, handsome? Or should I guess?"

His gaze moved between my eyes, a little panic behind his, mixed with something else. "It sounds so fucking childish, I hate myself."

I waited for him to continue. He puffed out a breath and traced my lips with his thumb—something he always did when he wanted to share something deep. His nostrils flared before he spoke. "I get two days a week with you. Sometimes an extra night. I want all that time to be with me. I'm a selfish prick, I know. But if you take on more responsibility, that's less time with me."

Endearing, annoying, but cute none the less. I gave him a little shove. "You knew the deal with me when you met me, Ry. I love my job."

"I know you do. It's admirable and I love that about you. But...do you have room to love someone, too?"

"What?" My throat became real dry, real fast. He spun me around so I faced the lake, my back pressed against his chest. "Ry, what did that mean?"

He rested his head on the spot right between my shoulder and neck, pressing a quick kiss on my favorite spot below my ear. It was about the only skin not covered with the scarf. "I have a proposition for you."

"Okay...I'm listening."

He held me there, the only sound his light breath by my ear. He kissed me three more times before he spun me around, carefully running his fingers over my bottom lip and cupping my neck. His eyes heated over and one of his eyes twitched—a sign he was either mad or worried. "I'm content with my career. You're content with yours. You work harder than anyone I know...even me. But here's the thing, the happiest part of my week is when I'm with you. I didn't know it was possible to be that happy. Waking up next to you, falling asleep with you, breakfast sex, after dinner sex, our movie marathons and your awful baking skills... I want all of it *all* the time."

"Hey—I'm not that bad at baking!" I cried but he gave me a knowing smirk and I smiled. "Okay, I am. But still. Rude."

"I enjoy watching you bake in your apron and how you squint when you read directions. The experience is my favorite part, not the dessert itself." He gave me my favorite smile, the one where his eyes crinkled on the sides. "See? Every second with you is my favorite and I hate saying goodbye to you every Sunday."

"I'm liking where this is going..." I bit my lip and tried to calm my racing heart. It beat so hard my ribs hurt. Rylan gave me a nervous smile and swallowed. Goddamn, he was cute. I reached out and took his fidgeting hand into mine. "Ry, what in the world are you nervous about?"

"Fuck, I don't know." He stared at me for two seconds before picking me up, my legs straddling him in broad daylight. "You're it for me. For life. Married or not, kids or not, that doesn't really matter to me. Just you. Move in with me. Live with me half the year in Chicago, and I'll live in this armpit city the other half. We can both work from home half the year. Let's just do it. I want you every fucking day, every fucking night and everything in between."

"Okay." I grinned at his shocked expression, my entire body humming with elation. He froze, not moving, and I pressed a kiss on his cold lips. It was simple, really. Everything made sense. We had shared a lot of things over the past five months, but not the three words he needed to hear. "Ry, I love you. How in the world did you think I'd say no?"

He blinked a couple of times before tensing his jaw. "You've never said it to me before."

"You haven't either, big guy. But love isn't just words. It's actions. It's promises. It's touches." I pressed another kiss on his mouth, using my tongue to deepen the kiss. We became *that* couple. Completely obsessed with each other and making out in the middle of a park. No fucks were given. "I know without a doubt you love me. You should know that, too."

"I was worried your job would come between us," he said in a quiet voice. He set me down but kept one hand on my shoulder. He ran one hand through his hair and gave me a hard look before smiling. "Holy shit. You said yes."

"I said *okay*. But pretty much the same thing."

He spun me around, letting out a glorious laugh and taking the final piece of my heart. He was all hard angles, smart tactical business decisions, but he had a soft side. And it was reserved for me and only me. "Goddamn it, I love you so fucking much, Fern."

I felt on fire with happiness. It was like I'd slipped into a hot tub—the cold wind disappeared and the location didn't matter. It was just him. "Was that your concern about the future?"

"Yes. And why I was being a little bit of an asshole about your job. I know what it means to you, to Kayla and the guys. It's a part of who you are and I'll never get in the way of that. But…when you work too much, I'm going to distract you. It might happen twice a day."

"I can live with that."

He gave me another soul-crushing kiss, our bodies humming in response. But then he pulled back and fumbled with something in his pocket. I gasped. *Holy shit.* His eyes widened in fear and he violently shook his head. "No. No. No. It's not—"

"What are you doing?" I asked, my nerves on high alert.

"It's not a ring. Fuck. I-I didn't want to rush anything." My confident man stuttered and fumbled with whatever was in his pocket. The image was endearing, his shaking hands and worried eyes making me fall for him even more.

I sighed in relief. It wasn't a proposal. "Okay."

He froze and searched my face for a good ten seconds before he tilted his adorable head to the side. "Did...did you *want* it to be one?"

"I don't know." It was the truth. Excitement and fear hit me at the same time. While I was relieved at not seeing a blue box in there, the thought didn't freak me out. Being married to him, being with him every day...yeah. I could see myself liking that. "Maybe?"

"Fern. You're killing me," he groaned and ran his hand over his face. "I bought you a stupid gift. It's just a keyring with the key to my place. Damn it. Not really that special compared to a ring."

I grinned and stared at the silver chain in his hands. My eyes stung—I blamed the wind—and I blinked away the moisture. How cute is he? *A keychain for me? God, I love him.* "It's perfect. Gimme."

He fidgeted with the box and handed me a Cubs keychain with a silver key. He dared me to argue with the Cubs logo...we'd had quite a few discussions about the better team, Cardinals or Cubs, and they'd always ended in a heated romp in bed, naked and agreeing to disagree. I held it in my hand and had never felt happier. "You know what's funny?"

"Dare I ask, what?"

"I had an extra copy of my key made last week. I figured, if I'm not home when you get in, it'd make sense for you to not wait around at a bar until I got home." I pocketed his key and stood on my tiptoes to wrap my arms around his shoulders. "We're always on the same page, aren't we? We're kinda perfect together."

"I messed it all up. I brought you your favorite whiskey and I was going to give it to you after the first two drinks. I'm not good with trying to surprise you," he said into my hair and squeezed me against him. "And need I remind you, you tried to break up with me at one point."

"Not the time for that, Ry." I snorted and let go of him. "So not the time after I confess we're perfect together."

He made a goofy face at me and tilted my chin. His hazel eyes turned serious and without warning, his entire posture changed. He went stiff and in a lowered voice, he asked, "What would you have said?"

I didn't understand the question at first, but the anxiety in his eyes told me. It was about the almost proposal. "I guess you'll have to ask me for real to find out."

"*Fern*," he warned but I shook my head at his tortured expression. He wasn't getting off this easily…not when I'd told him seconds ago we were on the same page. "Give me a clue."

"For such an intelligent guy, you have your slow moments." I kept walking down the path and stifled my laughter. He jogged up to me and picked me up, hauling me over his shoulder. "Rylan!"

"Yes or no. Or even a maybe. I need one of the above words said before I put you down."

"Are you bullying me into marriage?"

"I'm doing what I need to do. As a CEO, you'll learn."

"I sure as hell hope you don't do this to the guys you work with. That has HR written all over it."

He set me down and pushed me up against one of the trees. His eyes burned. Having all that passion directed at me wasn't fair. His amused expression was so goddamn sexy. "You're such a smart ass."

"How does Mrs. Smart Ass Cirula sound?"

He tensed again, a smile forming before a frown took its place. "I'm going to need you to be real clear, Fern."

"For Christ's sake, Moneybags. When you do ask me, because I'm not letting this be our story, where you practically kidnapped me in a park for an answer, I will most likely say *sure*."

"Just *sure*?" He placed his hands on either side of my face, cornering me from escaping. "We can barter orgasms if that helps."

"It won't hurt. I'll say that." I grabbed his jacket again and closed the distance between our mouths. I kissed him deeply, bringing him to the point I knew he would lose control. Then I pulled back, gave him the sexiest look I could and said, "I'm *all* in, Mr. Cirula."

* * * *

It took twelve hours for him to place a perfect turquoise box on the bed next to me. It took me less than one second to say yes.

The jewel was the color of whiskey, not so different from the color of his eyes. He got down on one knee and asked me those four words I hadn't been sure I'd ever agree to and I barely got the word out before he hauled me into the bedroom, where he showed me for the next two hours how good our life would be together.

Want to see more from this author? Here's a taster for you to enjoy!

Out of the Park: Evening the Score
Jaqueline Snowe

Excerpt

"Shut the fuck up. *The* baseball-playing star of my fantasies Gideon Titan?" Spit left my mouth and my pulse raced at the thought of that perfect specimen of a man. His poster hung in my room. He had starred in my dreams more than a handful of times. His eyes, abs and smile…I shivered. Wishes did come true. The receptionist at the Los Soles stadium gawked at me and I held up a hand. "Forgive my language. But please clarify. Who will I be coaching with again?"

Her gaze darted to the door as a blush crept up her neck. "Uh, Gideon Titan. He's volunteering for the season for the fourteen and under baseball team. You're paired together."

"Cool." *Ohmigod.* "Thank you." I tried my best to remain calm and smiled while she printed off the schedule. She chewed on her bottom lip so damn much I wanted to smack her. I couldn't be the first person to lose their shit at the chance to meet Gideon Titan.

He defined the term masculine. He put all men to shame. For a baseball-lovin' southwest chick, he was it. When he was in full form, he was the epitome of perfection. Even with his injury and slight limp, I would take any invitation he offered. I left her desk with the practice schedule, reading about the forty games within four months, four games a week after two weeks of full practice.

Fucking Jade. Amazing, beautiful Jade. I called my pseudo-boss from the non-profit I had volunteered at for the last four years. She was my best friend, mentor and the version of a sister I'd thought my real sisters would be. She answered on the first ring her voice cheery. "Lo?"

"Gideon Titan."

Jade's breathy laugh traveled through the phone. "Surprise?"

"Hell, yeah. Best surprise ever. When I asked to get involved with youth sports, I was thinking more like pee-wee soccer. Not baseball. How did you do this?" The fresh air hit my face as I barged through the exit and I couldn't contain my grin. November in Phoenix had perfect weather—I intended to enjoy every drop of it.

"Well, I know a guy who knows a guy...plus, you've put a lot of work into our programs that focus on high school kids. You're great with them and this will be a good fit. You can talk about the dangers of texting and driving and get to coach one-on-one with Gideon Titan. I see this as a win-win."

The stab of pain came and went—I was used to the wave of grief whenever Justin crossed my mind. It got easier to not react to it. I cleared my throat and wiped my suddenly sweaty palms on my jeans. "Thanks for thinking of me for this. I'm grateful. And hello? Gideon. Freaking. Titan."

"Yeah. I heard he can be a real asshole, but I want every detail."

My brain wasn't in the right place to fully comprehend her words. I laughed it off. With a face like Gideon's, he could ramble on and on about stupid, irrelevant information and I'd still be happy. "You misheard it. I'm sure they meant to say he's a hot piece of ass."

Jade sighed, ignoring me. *Typical Jade.* "Anyway, crazy. We need to talk about that job offer that is still unanswered."

My throat closed and I let out an awkward grunt. "Mm, yeah. Sure."

"I'll let you go enjoy your moment to think about Gideon, but I need an answer, Fi. See you at the office soon?"

"Yup." I hung up, took a deep breath and started the drive to the shitty two-bedroom apartment I'd moved into a month ago with a former co-worker. I'd made enough the two years before, waitressing at an IHOP, and had saved every last penny to be able to live on my own my senior year. I adored my mom and my childhood home but shit—I needed to cut the cord and live my life. Her meddling personality got in the way, despite her good intentions. I wasn't a bitch, but I wanted to be independent even if it killed me. Yeah—I had a stubborn thing going and I was damn proud of it.

Jade's words weighed heavy on me the entire drive. Volunteering at Texting Too Late had started out small to help me cope with Justin's death. But it had grown into more. Once a month had become twice, and twice a week had become almost daily. The foundation was amazing and it gave me a fulfillment I needed to deal with the guilt, but could I accept a full-time position knowing damn well every day would remind me of him, and my secret?

I gripped the wheel tighter and scoffed at all the couples holding hands. *What the fuck? It's like noon on a Tuesday – why are they just strolling down our shitty street?* I parked in the covered carport, spying Michelle's Toyota, and checked my phone before heading into our modest place.

Jade: You would get to see me every day.

Jade: Diane knows you kick ass with all the money stuff I avoid.

Fiona: Keep the compliments coming. It's good for my ego.

Jade: You could pick the music station?

Fiona: I would choose 2000s R&B and it's still a maybe.

I pocketed my phone and pulled my hair up into a ponytail before walking inside. I was quite proud of the way I handled donations to TTL and that our rating had gone up in the past three months. I allocated about fifteen percent of all donations for maintenance, freelance work and advertising, but Jade had proposed moving it to twenty and keeping me on full-time with pay. Diane – the president and founder – agreed.

It had insurance, great benefits and a good salary for a non-profit. I would work with Jade, who was pretty fucking awesome, and have a job on the table before graduating.

But…*Justin.*

Nah. Not today, grief. I straightened my shoulders, pushing down the negative spiral I was sure to have. I avoided feelings. Tied up, sewed shut. I hadn't had a relationship that amounted to more than awesome, gravity-defying sex since I was eighteen, but that didn't really count, and I was okay with it. Sex was easy. Attention was easy. Feelings were not. Feelings did not lead to happiness. I came across as wild, reckless or cold to most, but it didn't bother me. It was safer, smarter and survival. Light rock music carried from our place and I plowed through our front door. I had news and Michelle Benning needed to hear it.

"Michelle. Get your ass out here right now."

"What is it?" She waltzed out of her room, just to the right of the kitchen. She wore the ugly blue apron and had her hair done up. We both had our secrets, our pasts that defined the core pieces of us. But I hadn't asked her what hers were, nor had she asked me. We enjoyed each other's company and I didn't require much more than that from my first roommate besides my mom.

"Guess who the fuck I got paired with to coach this team. Guess." I plopped onto our long-standing burgundy couch. It had been a family piece and my mom had given it to us. It smelled like an old basement, of stale popcorn with a mix of lemon furniture polish. I loved it. Michelle ran her manicured red nails over her chin, humming in thought.

"My mind is blank. Tell me."

"Gideon Titan." I smirked, pulling up a picture of him on my phone. "*The* Gideon Titan."

"Fuck me sideways." She snatched the phone out of my hands. "I want to sit on his face."

"Girl, join the club. I want him to sit on my face." I fanned myself with my free hand. "I have to send him an email, or reach out to him somehow. Practices are four times a week! Then, forty games."

"I hate you." Her dark brown eyes widened, her hand going to her heart. "I'm not one of those jealous bitches. But I could cut you right now."

I snickered. "I don't blame you. Here, will you help me type out an email to him? Or should I call? What do you think?"

She took the schedule from my hands and skimmed the bottom line — *contact me for details.* She pursed her lips. "He left a number and email. What would you rather do?"

"It makes more sense to text, right?" Nerves took over. I would be texting someone whose face was plastered all over our city. *Wow. But what if he's driving?*

"I think so. If this wasn't Gideon Titan but some random person, you would text, right?"

"I'd rather call. I'd want to talk about logistics and division of coaching duties. It'd be easier to talk than type." I wiped my palms on my jeans. "Shit."

"Girl, this is insane. Call now. I want to hear his voice." She grasped my hand, with her face a little too happy, a little too eager. I couldn't blame her, though. My excitement and nerves took center stage and the reality of the situation had me stiff. "Call."

"Okay, okay!" I skimmed the informational sheet the woman had given me and his number sat at the bottom. Gideon Titan's number. I dialed it, hesitating for a second before pressing call. Then it rang. "Shit. Ah!"

It rang three times, each tone causing more sweat to form on my brow. The fourth ring, he answered.

"It's Gideon."

His voice was rough and strangled, but my body reacted to it anyway. My legs clenched together, the deep tone affecting me way too much. Michelle said something to get my attention and I cleared my throat. "Hi, Gideon Titan. My name is Fiona — "

"Who fucking gave you my number?"

His sudden verbal attack made me jump. My tremulous voice gave me away, I was sure. "Los Soles, sir."

"Why?" Something shuffled in the background, the accusation clear as day. "What do you want?"

"We-we got paired to coach the fourteen-blue team." *Goddamn my nerves.*

"Christ." He released a long, aggravated sigh. "I don't need another coach. Tell them you can't do it and never call this number again."

Then he hung up.

The first spark of anger began in my stomach. It worked its way up to my chest, then to my neck. I wanted to murder this guy. He was an asshole of epic proportions. Michelle's eyes were the size of small saucers.

"Did he for real just do that?" Her brittle voice matched mine.

"Yeah. The fucker hung up on me." I fisted the paper into a crumpled ball. "Fuck him."

I hit redial, his rough voice answering the same. "Listen, asshole. I'm coaching with you. I want this opportunity. So fuck off. I'll see you at the first practice."

Then I hung up.

"Oh my god. What did I do?" I threw my phone onto the small coffee table. Michelle's face remained unmoving, as though my actions had frozen time. Whoever cusses at Gideon Titan?

"When is the first practice?" she asked.

I unfolded the paper, glancing at the date and times. "In five days. That should be enough time for everyone to cool down, yeah?"

"Sure, hon." Michelle got up, shaking her head at me a little bit. "I knew I liked you for a reason. Your balls are bigger than most men I know."

I laughed. "Then you aren't around decent guys. Ball size is everything."

She cackled, shouldering her purse and reapplying lipstick. "Balls are a deal breaker for me."

"Dude, I know." I leaned farther back into the couch, wishing it would swallow me up. Regret and embarrassment would hit me later, with Michelle at work and no one to distract me. "I've said it all the time, but balls are weird. Guys have to have them, but where do they go when they ride a bike?"

"Right! Or when they sit? Do they squish them to the side or flatten them?"

"How can they cross their legs?" I added. "And why must they touch them all the damn time? And do the reach-down-then-smell-their-fingers thing?"

"Why do they ball tap each other? I don't mind a titty twister now and again, but I don't greet my friends with a boob grab every time."

I laughed—Michelle had a great point. "I mean, the thought they walk around with a stick hanging out boggles my mind. But add two squishy sacks of skin next to it? Why?" I closed my eyes, thoughts of balls and penises overtaking my mind.

Michelle snickered and headed toward the door. She had to work and the thought of doing homework alone depressed me. "I'll be home later than normal. I might be staying until breakfast."

"Damn, well, be safe. I'll be here thinking about balls."

"God." She shook her head. "I'm glad we're roomies. See you."

She shut the door and I smiled. I liked Michelle as much as I could like someone outside my family. Hope blossomed in my chest that maybe, just maybe, I could let her in.

Home of Erotic Romance

Sign up for our newsletter and find out about all our romance book releases, eBook sales and promotions, sneak peeks and FREE romance books!

About the Author

Jaqueline Snowe lives in Arizona where the 'dry heat' really isn't that bad. She enjoys making lists with colorful Post-it notes and sipping coffee all day. She has been a custodian, a waitress, a landscaper, a coach and a teacher. Her life revolves around binge-watching Netflix, her two dogs who don't realize they aren't humans and her wonderful baseball-loving husband.

Jaqueline loves to hear from readers. You can find her contact information, website details and author profile page at https://www.totallybound.com

www.ingramcontent.com/pod-product-compliance
Lightning Source LLC
Chambersburg PA
CBHW020412180626
46812CB00003B/937